For Maria —

D1367961

# TO BEAR AN
# IRON KEY

## JACKIE MORSE KESSLER

**Month9Books**

**Month9Books**

*For the incredible Renée Barr,*
*who's read everything I've ever written:*
*This one's for you!*

# PART 1: FIVE YEARS AGO

## BEGINNINGS

# A KINDRED SPIRIT

She sat alone in the small room, like a storybook princess trapped inside a witch's cottage. But the girl with curly black hair, which draped down to her thighs when she stood, was no princess. Bromwyn, called Darkeyes, was herself a witch, and she was quite certain that one day she would be able to perform magical feats that none had ever seen before. Her power would dazzle and astound, and everyone in the village, from her mother to the mayor, would bow their heads and murmur "Wise One" as she walked past, and they would all love her forever and let her do whatever she wished.

Yes, Bromwyn was a witch. But she was also an eleven-year-old girl who had been grounded by her grandmother, and she was indeed trapped inside a witch's cottage. Her grandmother had cast a spell on the small house to keep Bromwyn tucked safely inside.

Try as she might, the girl could not escape.

So she sat in her bedroom, and she sulked, and she thought rather evil things about her grandmother—most of which were true, but even so, she had no business thinking them.

Her grandmother's spell, strong as it was, couldn't muffle the raucous laughter coming from the forest. The cottage rested on the outskirts of the Allenswood, and Bromwyn usually enjoyed hearing the birdsong and tree-chatter as she performed her daily chores as her grandmother's apprentice. But now, every bit of noise from the woods felt like a blow to her heart. From the sounds of it, the fey seemed to be enjoying themselves immensely. They were probably dancing and telling riddles and playing tag. And flying. Bromwyn sighed wistfully as she imagined what it would be like to spin in the air, held aloft by fey magic. Witches might be powerful, but none of them could fly, not even her grandmother.

She closed her eyes and smiled as she pictured herself aloft, her bare feet far above the ground as she moved to the music of the moon and the stars. She could almost pretend that she was dancing across the sky ...

... but then she opened her eyes and saw that she was still trapped in her grandmother's small house, and her smile vanished. She should be at her grandmother's side, taking part in the Midsummer Festival! She should be dancing and laughing with the fey!

But no. She was stuck inside the cottage, all because she had spoken her mind. It wasn't as if she'd been rude. She had merely insisted, quite politely, that she deserved to know why she wasn't allowed to greet the fey.

"What you deserve," Niove Whitehair had replied, "is to be so sore that you would not sit for a week. In this house, you obey my rules. I said you cannot go, and that is the rule."

"Rules, rules, rules," Bromwyn had said—again, politely. "You always give me rules and never give me reasons!"

"The only reason you need is this: If you are to continue as my apprentice, you will obey my rules. Without question. You need boundaries, girl. You need protection." And then Niove had spelled the cottage.

Thinking about her grandmother's words now, Bromwyn scowled. Protection—what utter nonsense. She was a witch! Her grandmother, of all people, should have known that witches didn't need protection from anything. Therefore, Bromwyn decided, "protection" was just an excuse for her grandmother to spoil all of her fun.

Outside the cottage, Midsummer rolled on.

When Bromwyn grew bored of sulking, she practiced her magic, creating cantrips that lit the small room in fitful bursts. Full of spark and spice, shreds of light whirled in the air, swirling with summer colors: fiery yellows and bright greens, velvety blues and haughty purples, all blooming lushly. But as vibrant as these lights were, as proud and full of life as they tried to be, they were merely cantrips, not meant to last. They died, gracefully and joyfully, burning themselves out within moments—never truly alive, never knowing that their brief existence was just a taste, a sip, a tease.

This did nothing for Bromwyn's mood.

Finally, full of longing and impotent rage, Bromwyn stamped her foot and declared, "I want out!"

"Nala wants in," a tiny voice answered.

Startled, Bromwyn turned to the window.

There, floating on the other side of the glass, was a creature barely the length of Bromwyn's little finger. The figure pressed against the window, peering in. A shock of blond hair crowned her head, and from beneath her choppy bangs, two piercingly blue eyes regarded Bromwyn. Dressed in a gown of miniscule flowers, she hovered, her gossamer wings flitting like a hummingbird's.

A pixie.

Bromwyn had been schooled by her grandmother about much of the fey; most she could name by rote, and she was familiar with many of their ways—you never called them "fairies," for one thing, and you never took anything from them without giving them something in return. But for all of her knowledge, she had never actually seen any of the fey, other than as illustrations in books. Only once a year did those magical creatures step into the world, and only to take part in the Midsummer Festival: Her grandmother witnessed their entrance at dusk, watched to ensure they didn't do anything terrible (or at least nothing too permanent) throughout the night, and then made them take their leave by dawn, locking the World Door behind them. Only her grandmother could decide when Bromwyn would be ready to greet the fey—which, the girl was starting to think, would be far closer to "never" than to "today." When Niove Whitehair decided something, that was that. Bromwyn couldn't go to greet the fey.

But nothing had stopped the fey from coming to greet *her*.

She grinned with delight. A real pixie was right there, outside the cottage! Bromwyn ran to the window and pressed her face against it.

Separated by glass and magic, the two stared at each other. The tiny creature stroked the window as if she could touch Bromwyn's cheek. The girl tried the window latch, but her hand was slapped away by her grandmother's spell.

Rubbing her sore fingers, she cried, "Let me out!"

The pixie cocked her head. "Big ward," she said, her voice clear even from the other side of the window. "Too big for Nala."

Bromwyn uttered a very un-witchlike word.

"Let Nala in," the pixie said. "The Whitehair is no fun. You would be fun, yes? We could play together. Let Nala in, witch girl. Let Nala in."

"If you could get in," Bromwyn said reasonably, "then I could get out. And I cannot get out."

"The Whitehair forces you to stay?"

Frustrated, Bromwyn nodded.

"Why?"

"She says that I need boundaries, that I need *protection*." She stamped her foot once again. "She thinks that I am still a baby!"

"A babe?" Nala pursed her lips as she floated. "You still suckle milk?"

Bromwyn wrinkled her nose. "Of course not. But Grandmother treats me like a baby. She will keep locking me up until I am as old as she is, and I will live my life without having any fun at all!"

"But why do you need protection? Are you not a witch like the Whitehair?"

"Thank you, yes, I am! And no, I do *not* need protection. But that does not matter to Grandmother. She decided that I cannot get out. And in *this* house," Bromwyn said, mimicking her grandmother's voice, "you obey Niove Whitehair's rules!"

"Rules." Nala sighed mournfully. "Always there are rules."

"Always rules," Bromwyn agreed with a sigh of her own. "And the most important rule is 'Never argue with Grandmother.'"

"We have rules, too, witch girl. Magic means rules. You and Nala, we are quite alike." Then the pixie brightened. "But your granddam, the Whitehair, she is not here at the moment."

Bromwyn pouted. "No. She is with your kin in the woods, having all sorts of fun." Then, with a touch of pride, she added, "My grandmother is the Guardian, you know."

"Oh, Nala knows. Often the King and Queen bespeak her name with much color and venom. Nala thinks," she added in a whisper, "that *they* think the Whitehair an equal, though they never say this, and certainly not to Nala."

Bromwyn considered Nala's words, then nodded. "Grandmother is the Wise One of our village. So I suppose she could be the equal of the King and Queen."

"Strong as she is," Nala said, her gemstone eyes twinkling with mischief, "she is not here at the moment. You cannot argue with her if she is not here, no?"

Bromwyn smiled in anticipation. "No."

"What was her rule to you tonight, witch girl? What were her

8

exact words that are keeping you bound within the abode?"

"Exact words ... " Bromwyn frowned as she remembered. "She said that nothing could enter the cottage without her leave, and that I could not escape." She spread her arms wide, taking in the entire room. "And I cannot. I tried the windows, the doors, the chimney, even the trap door under the floorboard in the kitchen, the one she thinks I do not know about. Everything is stuck tight."

"Stuck tight," Nala said, nodding. "Nala cannot enter: that is a rule. You cannot escape: that is another rule. But you *can* simply leave."

Bromwyn blinked. "I can?"

Nala grinned. "Surely. She did not say you could not *leave* the abode. She said you could not *escape* the abode. So do not try to escape. Just walk out. The rule is not broken, and the ward remains intact."

Biting back a premature cry of hope, Bromwyn walked out of her small bedroom and into the kitchen, heading for the door that led out into the backyard. By the wooden door, Bromwyn paused, her hand hovering over the knob as Nala had hovered by her window.

What would happen if she broke her grandmother's ward? The name Niove Whitehair was spoken in whispers by even the bravest of souls. Her magic was powerful, and she was feared by most and respected by all. And she had no sense of humor.

Swallowing, Bromwyn tried not to think of possible consequences. Instead, she focused on the pixie's words.

Aloud, she said, "Grandmother did not say I could not leave the cottage. She said I could not escape. I am not breaking her rule. I am not trying to escape. I am simply leaving."

Taking a deep breath, Bromwyn turned the knob and opened the door.

With a laugh, she leapt outside. Her long hair billowed around her like a cape as she turned in circles, thrilling in the feel of the wind on her face, of the spongy grass beneath her bare feet. Her dress fanned out as she spiraled across her grandmother's lawn, and her delighted giggles filled the air, momentarily drowning out the chortles from the Midsummer Festival deep within the woods.

The sound of clapping brought her to a halt. Nala continued applauding as she darted by Bromwyn's head. "You are free, witch girl!"

"I am! Thank you, friend Nala! Thank you for your help!"

"Rules are easy to follow," the pixie said with a shrug, "if you are certain of the words. This is why you must always be careful of what you say. Now come! Let us play! Catch Nala if you can, witch girl!"

So Bromwyn gave chase, laughing as she ran after Nala's tiny flying form. They darted through the Allenswood, Nala flitting between branches heavy with green foliage and Bromwyn capering after her on foot, skirting roots and other obstacles as best she could. After tripping for a third time, Bromwyn used her magic to create globes brighter than any candle and peppered them among the trees. She did not worry about accidentally setting the leaves afire; these were merely illusions of light, giving off brightness but no heat. That was the Way of Sight, and it was Bromwyn's path of magic.

"The witch girl cannot see in the dark?" Nala asked, fluttering near Bromwyn's head.

"The witch girl is not a cat," Bromwyn declared. "Though she is about to catch you!" She swatted at Nala, barely missing the pixie's wings.

Laughing, the two set off once again, Nala buzzing around trees and Bromwyn chasing after. It didn't matter that they went deeper and deeper into the woods; where Nala went, Bromwyn would follow. She would catch the pixie, and then it would be Nala's turn to catch her. They would spend the night playing tag, Bromwyn decided, and it would be the beginning of their own annual tradition. Let her grandmother have the rest of the fey; Bromwyn would have Nala. Soon they would become the best of friends, and over the years, they would share secrets and stories, and they would discover new things together. Bromwyn knew that she had made a lifelong friend this night.

Magic could be lonely, but now that didn't matter. Bromwyn had found a kindred spirit.

Exuberant from her stolen freedom and new friendship, Bromwyn didn't realize that she had stumbled upon the Midsummer Festival until she nearly careened into the stoic form of her grandmother.

# A WISH FOR A WITCH

Skidding to a halt, Bromwyn stared up at Niove Whitehair.

Taller than almost everyone, and older than anyone, her grandmother loomed like a dead tree—frightening, bent, radiating menace. Like Bromwyn's, her hair was uncut, and it draped over her shoulders and down her back to her ankles, thicker than any cloak could be, like cold moonlight against the severity of her black shawl and dress. Her gaze bore into Bromwyn, and the young witch flinched from the combination of rage and disappointment she saw simmering there.

"Bromwyn Elmindrea Lucinda Moon," Niove hissed, her voice like death, "what are you doing out of the cottage?"

Upon hearing her full name, Bromwyn knew that she was in more trouble than she could have ever imagined. In a blink, the globes she had created disappeared. Yet there was still ample light;

her grandmother had seen to that. Pinpoints of luminescence twinkled in the trees, as if stars had been caught in the boughs. It was a beautiful effect, and under other circumstances, Bromwyn would have clapped her hands in pleasure.

Instead, she bit her lip. Then she admitted, "I was playing with a pixie."

Now Bromwyn clearly heard the shouts and laughter and buzzing of the fey. She risked a glance past her grandmother to the clearing behind her, and her gaze fixed upon the Hill, standing with its circle of stones at the top.

Even with the looming danger of her enraged grandmother, Bromwyn couldn't help but think: *I am here! Midsummer is dancing around me, and I am here in the center of it!*

Above the stones on the Hill, the outline of a door—or, more accurately, a Door—shimmered with fey magic. The World Door was open, as it always was during the Midsummer Festival, and swarming around it were hundreds of flying creatures. Some were as small as Nala, flitting between leaves and plants, playing hide-and-go-seek with the birds. Others were human-sized, flying heavily with their thin wings. Some were frighteningly large. But no matter their size, each of them looked the same: a mop of blond hair, shockingly blue eyes, swathed in flowers instead of clothes. Some were men and some were women—and some looked rather like both—but all of them were alike. A few of them pointed at her; others waved, beckoning her to come play with them. She tried to find Nala, but it was impossible to spy one pixie amid the fey horde.

"Bromwyn," her grandmother snarled, "pay attention!"

Bromwyn gasped, then looked at Niove. It was one thing to ignore her grandmother's ire. It was another thing altogether to get caught doing so. Bromwyn's cheeks burned with embarrassment.

"You are not 'playing with a pixie.'" Niove's eyes narrowed. "What you are doing, girl, is disobeying me."

Disobeying. In other words, she was breaking the rules.

Bromwyn chewed her lip as she looked down at her bare feet. Around her, she could hear the fey whispering, and they seemed to say:

*Rules. Your granddam is full of rules. You will never be free of them.*
*You will never be free of her.*

Bromwyn's nostrils flared. By Fire and Air, she was sick of all of the rules. "Do not do this." "Never say that." "Grandmother is always right." Well, enough. No matter how her grandmother treated her, she was not a baby—she could make her own decisions.

She lifted her chin boldly. "I am *not* disobeying. You forbade me to escape the cottage. And I did *not* escape. I walked out."

"You," Niove said, "are being insolent. And I will not have it, girl. Not from you, and not now. Get back to the cottage before they notice you."

"No!" Bromwyn folded her arms across her chest. "I want to stay!"

Her grandmother's eyes flashed fire, but Bromwyn refused to look away. Let Niove be angry; Bromwyn was angry too. And when she wished, Bromwyn could outstare a stone. So she held her grandmother's fierce gaze with the dark eyes for which she was called.

But as she looked into her grandmother's eyes, Bromwyn saw a gleam there that had nothing to do with rage or disappointment. What she saw was fear.

Stuff and nonsense; what could possibly scare Niove Whitehair?

Quietly, urgently, her grandmother said, "Go. We will discuss this later, you and I. But for Nature's sake, girl, go. *Now.*"

Her grandmother's words were a command, and Bromwyn started to obey before she forced her feet to remain still. Her heart beating much too fast, she whispered, "No."

"Hail, Whitehair!"

The voice that called was deep and booming, and it thundered through the woods.

Niove stiffened, and Bromwyn heard her mutter a curse that should have burned off her ears. The girl turned to see who called.

Fascinated, she watched as two figures floated toward them. The smaller one, a woman, was clothed in flowers and silk, and her long green hair shone with diamonds. Holding her hand, the other figure, a blond man, wore blue silks and a cape of flowers, with a crown of silver on his brow. They came to a halt in midair, hovering over Bromwyn. Unlike the other fey, these two did not have wings. Around them, the other fey creatures, large and small alike, settled down to watch the encounter.

Bromwyn felt hundreds of pairs of eyes upon her, and it was all she could do not to squirm.

"Pray tell, my lady Guardian," the man said with a smile, "who is this girl child by your skirts?"

"My lord and lady of the fey," her grandmother answered tightly, as if the words cut her mouth, "I present to you my granddaughter Bromwyn, called Darkeyes."

The woman laughed, and her voice would have made nightingales jealous. "She is yours, this witch girl? What delight! I thought it would be a human's age before we saw another Guardian."

"She is too young to be a Guardian," the man said, his blue eyes brimming with mirth. "She is too young to be a proper witch, for that matter. A witchling, perhaps."

"Make your manners, girl," Niove hissed, clouting Bromwyn on the shoulder. "You stand before the King and Queen of the fey."

Bromwyn curtseyed awkwardly. "Greetings, rulers of the fair folk," she said, and she was proud that her voice didn't catch. "May Nature bless you always."

The King roared laughter, which echoed in the mouths of the watching fey.

Bromwyn felt heat rise in her cheeks, and she nervously bit her lip.

The Queen smiled. "A lovely wish, witch girl." Her voice was enticing, and it made Bromwyn think of sugar cookies. "Of course, Nature already blesses the fey, so your appeal was unnecessary. But you are young. You will learn the proper etiquette among our Court." The Queen glanced at Niove slyly, as if she knew something and was not going to tell.

Niove said, "Now that she has made herself known, it is time for my granddaughter to return home. The girl needs her rest."

"The girl needs to have some fun before she takes her leave of our esteemed company," the King said, extending his hand to Bromwyn. "Come, witchling. Do me the honor of a dance."

Her heart beating wildly, she was about to reach out to him when her grandmother murmured, "If you go to him, girl, I cannot protect you."

But Bromwyn was a witch. She didn't need protection.

With a grin that was half joyous and half fearful, she took the hand of the fey King. Her body tingled, and for a moment she saw an amber glow around her hand. Then her feet left the ground. Held aloft at the King's side, she floated, her hair a curling curtain that rippled down to the backs of her thighs.

Smiling, the King pulled her close, then took her other hand in his.

Stepping on nothing, they began to dance.

Feeling her breath stick in her throat, Bromwyn tried to swallow. But as she moved with the King, her fear gave way to rapture. She was flying! With each step, she felt the air itself cushion her feet, embracing her body with gentle care. The King led her along the sky, and with a grin that ate her face, she followed step for step.

Far below them, the Midsummer Festival continued.

"You are quite the witchling," the King said. His eyes shone like sapphires, and his smile was warm, inviting. On his brow, his crown caught the moonlight. "You need not stay under the confines of your grandmother. The Whitehair places so many restrictions upon you. I can sense your darkest heart. You wish to be free."

Giddy from her magical dance, Bromwyn agreed.

Smiling, the King said, "I could give you your wish, young Darkeyes. Come with me and my lady Queen. Join us as we go through the World Door at dawn to return to our land, where you would be our daughter. In our land, you will have no rules. In our land, you may run and play and dance among the stars as much as you wish. What say you?"

She wanted to say "yes," more than anything.

But even through the joy of her air-swept dance, she saw something hungry poking at the King's smile. And she remembered Nala's words, which had been so mournful at the time and now seemed to be a warning:

*We have rules, too, witch girl. Magic means rules.*

*Always there are rules.*

Carefully, Bromwyn said, "But there are rules to magic. And you, my lord—you *are* magic. How could I have no rules in your land? How could there be nothing expected of me?"

"I am King," he said firmly, "and if I say you would have no rules, that would be truth. In return, I would require only one thing: You must love me with all of your heart."

No rules. No one telling her what she could or could not do.

No one telling her "no."

No one—except the King.

He tipped her backward. Dipped in his arms, she again saw the hunger in his smile.

"Thank you, my lord," she finally answered after he raised her back upright. "But I must say no."

His eyes darkened. In a voice like the silk he wore, he asked, "Are you certain, witchling? Once refused, this offer will never be made again. Think carefully."

Bromwyn did not need to think carefully—the rage that stormed in the King's eyes was all the confirmation she needed.

"I am sorry if I have angered you," she said politely. "But I still must say no."

The King's hands tightened around hers, and she felt how easily he could crush her bones.

"Others have given their souls to dance with the fey," he said. "Others have sacrificed their lives for just a hint of the wonders of my land. And you refuse me?"

"Yes, my lord," Bromwyn whispered.

Sapphire eyes glinting coldly, the King said, "If you tell me why you have refused, and if I accept your answer, then I will give you your life. If you do not answer, or if your answer displeases me, I will release your hands and watch you fall to your death."

Bromwyn bit her lip as she realized just how high up they were. If the King dropped her, she would die.

Her grandmother had been right: A witch needed protection after all.

Trying not to sound as scared as she felt, she said, "With my grandmother, I know what the rules are. I know when I am breaking them." She took a deep breath and continued: "But if I followed you back to your land, my lord, I would never know what the rules would be. Because, my lord, if I loved you with all of my heart, your wish would be my command. I would not be able to say no."

The King stared at her long and hard, and Bromwyn thought that he was going to drop her.

"I am sorry, my lord," she said in a small voice. "But no thank you."

There was a long pause. Finally, the King barked out a laugh.

"Well spoken, witchling. I have offered you my land, which you have refused. In return, you have offered me your life, which I have refused. The scales are balanced. Come. Let us return to the Whitehair."

Bromwyn didn't understand his words; she had never offered him her life. Then again, grownups rarely made sense. Besides, she knew enough to keep her mouth shut.

They floated down, and down, and finally Bromwyn's feet touched the ground. One look at her grandmother told her just how furious Niove was with her. That was fine. Bromwyn would rather face her grandmother's wrath than the King's displeasure. Her grandmother was powerful, and she was strict, and she could be scary. But the King was scarier.

Bromwyn hugged her grandmother fiercely, and when she felt Niove's hands press gently on her shoulders, she nearly sobbed in relief.

"My lord King," said Niove, "my granddaughter must take her leave. She is tired."

"Indeed," the King replied. "I believe my dance has exhausted her." He laughed like summer thunder. "She is clever, Whitehair. You have your hands full."

"I know," Niove said darkly. "Make your manners, girl, and go back to the cottage. No arguments."

"Yes, Grandmother," Bromwyn answered as meekly as she could. Turning to face the King and Queen, she curtsied deeply. "My lord and lady of the fey, good night to you. And thank you especially, my lord."

"Never let it be said that the King of the fey is not generous," he said with a wry smile. "Good night, witchling. I am certain we will meet again."

The Queen laughed softly. "If my husband the King is certain, then it will be so. Until next time, Darkeyes."

"Go," Niove said to Bromwyn. Lower, she added, "And you had better believe that we will be discussing this in the morning, girl."

Bromwyn ran home. No fey creature, pixie or otherwise, followed her.

In the morning, shortly after the World Door had closed and the Midsummer Festival ended, Bromwyn and her grandmother had a very lengthy discussion. Niove punctuated her points with swift-handed swats. After, Bromwyn was so sore that she knew she wouldn't sit comfortably for a week, and her tongue had been spelled to silence—for how long, her grandmother had refused to say.

But even tender-bottomed and mute, as well as once again trapped inside her grandmother's cottage, Bromwyn had never

21

more appreciated that she had rules.

As Nala had told her, rules were easy to follow if you were certain of the words.

*And,* Bromwyn thought with a smile, *once you are certain of the words, you can figure out how to bend the rules without breaking them.*

And *that* promised to be a lot of fun.

# PART 2: NOW

# THE KEY

# HASTY WORDS

"Bromwyn, stand still!"

"I *am* standing still."

"Restless feet," her mother warned, "make my fingers nervous. I would prefer not to stick you with a pin. Blood would stand out horribly against the white."

Bromwyn forced her feet to stop fidgeting.

Her mother continued hemming the billowing silk dress that hung from Bromwyn like a sack; she was thin and gangly, and clothing preferred to swim on her rather than to be worn properly. Atop her head, her heavy curls of black hair towered in piles and braids, threatening to spill down her back and legs. Her mother had insisted that Bromwyn pin her hair back. The last thing she needed, Jessamin had said, was for thick tresses to be sewn into her daughter's wedding gown.

"Witches are not supposed to marry," Bromwyn said for the millionth time. By her feet, her mother continued working with the hem as her daughter complained. "Witches are supposed to have consorts."

"Witches," said Jessamin, "are supposed to listen to their mothers."

Bromwyn felt her temper flare, and she attempted to catch and cage it before it flew away. When her rages came upon her, nothing good happened. Two years ago, she had gotten very angry over something either real or imagined—she did not recall what it was, which really didn't matter; the result had been the same. Bromwyn had used her magic in anger.

Worse, she had used her magic against her mother.

Even now, Bromwyn could see the aftereffect of her rash deed. Her mother's hands, which used to be so deft and certain, held a slight tremor as she carefully hemmed the white silk gown. And when Jessamin read her cards to the villagers, there were times she would tremble so badly, it was as if her hands had a stutter. Usually, she was able to use the impediment to her advantage; customers tended to believe that Mistress Cartomancer was overcome by the power of her reading, and they would lean closer to catch her words of wisdom and guidance as Bromwyn, unnoticed in the corner, would watch, half disgusted by their gullibility, half dismayed that her mother was forced to play such a demeaning role.

*It is your own fault*, she told herself, staring at her mother's shaking hands.

Two years ago, Bromwyn had enchanted Jessamin's looking glass. She had done so quickly and quietly, barely needing to whisper the words from her Way of Sight. Her mother, who had been so furious with her, hadn't noticed. Or perhaps she had noticed, but had also assumed that her daughter would not do something so rash.

And yet, Bromwyn had.

When her mother had turned and caught her own reflection in the spelled glass, she had seen herself as a crone, old and bent. Held rapt by the image of her decaying body, Jessamin had frozen, transfixed by the illusion.

Bromwyn remembered smiling at that moment. Her mother had always been a proud one, and seeing herself defeated by time would do her good. Bromwyn remembered thinking that too.

And then the unthinkable had happened: Illusion transformed into something with substance. The magic, unsettled on the mirror, leeched onto and into her mother, and Bromwyn had watched in horror as Jessamin's body began to age—slowly, at first, and then with alarming speed.

With a defiant cry, Bromwyn had quickly unraveled the spell before it could take effect on Jessamin completely. But the magic, once cast, needed to go somewhere; in her panic, Bromwyn channeled it into her own body. That had been a mistake. She should have directed it into the dirt floor, or into the embers in the stone hearth, even into the air itself—any of the elements of Nature would have sufficed. But she'd reacted without thinking; all she had known at that urgent moment was that she had to do *something.*

All of her grandmother's lessons and warnings about the untamed strength of unraveled magic could not have prepared her for the wrenching pain she had felt as raw power racked her body—and that pain was nothing compared with the terror stitched onto Jessamin's weathered face.

Driven by equal parts fury and fear, Bromwyn had wrestled the wild magic and finally bested it, dispelling it into harmless wisps of smoke that soon evaporated. The mirror shattered, and Jessamin was restored to herself, unmarred ... except for the tremor that possessed her hands even now, two years later.

Her mother had long since forgiven her. Though Jessamin herself was no longer a witch, she had told Bromwyn that she remembered the temptations of youth. "The only things that mix more poorly than magic and youth," Jessamin Moon liked to say with a knowing smile, "are oil and water." But since that fateful day, there were times when Bromwyn would catch her mother glancing at her with something close to fear in her eyes.

Bromwyn did not like to think about that; mothers should not fear their daughters.

But Niove Whitehair—whom Bromwyn was convinced had never been young, let alone known the temptations of youth—was not one to overlook such a terrible trespass. Casting magic in anger? And against her own mother? Unspeakable. *Unforgivable.*

To emphasize her point, she had cursed her granddaughter.

Over her sixteen years in the village of Loren, Bromwyn had heard the residents speak in hushed tones about gypsy curses, how they were the worst things that could ever be set upon a person; that was why, she was sure, the villagers always welcomed the traveling folk whenever they visited to entertain and peddle their wares. But she knew that the gypsies had learned the art of the curse from witches.

Now, as Jessamin put the final touches on the hem of her daughter's wedding gown, Bromwyn recited the words of the curse to herself, once again looking for a way to unravel its power and rid herself of it once and for all.

*When anger rages within your heart*
*And you speak words in haste*
*Those very words will prompt events*
*That will serve to give you a taste*
*Of resentment and bitterness and icy fear*
*Until you are ready to mend*
*The rift of rage with self-sacrifice:*
*Love brings this curse to its end.*

Love. Fire and Air, how was she supposed to find love when she was forced to marry against her will?

But that, too, was her fault. She was certain that she had brought about her own upcoming marriage when she'd accidentally evoked the curse last year. Her temper had once again gotten the better of her, and once again with her mother. It had been over Bromwyn's tendency to walk barefoot everywhere—which, as her mother had pointed out, was something only children did, and never mind the filth that seemed to be permanently etched onto Bromwyn's feet. Jessamin had gone on about it being "unbecoming for a witch" and so forth, and Bromwyn, exhausted from a grueling day of magical study with her grandmother, had shouted: "What would *you* know about being a witch?"

The very next day, Jessamin announced that Bromwyn was to marry Brend Underhill, Nick Ironside's apprentice blacksmith, upon her seventeenth birthday.

Even now, as Bromwyn stood shrouded in her bridal gown, the thought of her impending wedding in a few months' time sent tendrils of cold rage through her body. She did not fear the thought of marriage, nor did it make her bitter. But she had never resented anything more in her life.

"There now," her mother said, pulling Bromwyn out of her dark thoughts. Jessamin sat back on her knees and looked critically at the white dress, which Bromwyn thought still fit her like a sack. "The length is right. Now if only you would be so kind as not to grow any taller until after your birthday, I would be most pleased."

Bromwyn bit back her anger and said nothing.

Her mother sighed. "It is not as bad as all that. Marriage can be a wonderful thing."

Bromwyn nearly choked on her tongue to keep from saying something she would dearly regret. What did her mother know of marriage? Jessamin's husband had died when Bromwyn was just a baby. Jessamin and Oren Moon had only a bare handful of years together; no one in the village even recalled that Mistress Cartomancer had ever been married. That, too, seemed to help her reputation as an esteemed card reader, for some reason that Bromwyn couldn't fathom.

"Brend is strong," her mother continued, "and he will do what is right. He will keep you safe."

"Safe from what?" Bromwyn blurted. "The ignorant people here who worship their invisible god?"

Jessamin frowned deeply. "Those ignorant people, as you call them, will be yours to care for, once your grandmother deems you worthy of the title 'Wise One.' Whether they are awed by your power or fear it, they are yours. Do not belittle them."

Bromwyn simmered.

"And even among the sheep, there can be a wolf lurking," her mother warned. "There are those even here who think that a witch is unnatural."

Bromwyn sniffed her derision. "That is ridiculous."

"It is also true. Those few small-minded villagers do not know any better, and they do not care to learn. They are to be pitied," Jessamin said. "But even as you pity them, you must take precaution. For now, you are safe; not even the smallest-minded man or woman here in Loren would willingly harm a child, not when the penalty is the Village Justice's axe. All they can do is look upon you with mistrust."

In her bridal gown, Bromwyn squirmed. Since she had become her grandmother's apprentice, she had felt such gazes upon her almost every day.

"But once you are seventeen and an adult, those same people might not think twice before they let you know just how unnatural they consider you to be. Witches can bleed like anyone else. You need protection. You need Brend's strength."

"Then let him be my consort," Bromwyn said, exasperated, "with no restrictions, no oaths that will bind us together for the rest of our lives!"

"Bromwyn—"

"Or let me choose my own consort, one whom I love!"

Her mother's face darkened. "You are to marry on your seventeenth birthday, and that is final."

"Then if I must marry, let me at least love the one sworn to my side! Or have you forgotten what love means?" Bromwyn clamped her mouth shut, hoping that her hasty words would not be enough to stir her grandmother's curse to life once again.

Jessamin whispered, "How dare you."

Bromwyn opened her mouth, then closed it when she saw the fury in her mother's eyes.

On her lap, Jessamin's hands balled into fists, and she lowered her voice as her knuckles whitened. "Do you truly think I have forgotten love? Do you think I prefer to be without your father? Do you think my life has been better with him gone all these years?"

Bromwyn's mouth went dry. "Mother, I—"

"Perhaps you have forgotten your father, Daughter, but I have not!" Jessamin's shout echoed in the small room. "Do not presume to lecture me about love! It is no longer my Way, but I have not forgotten its touch!"

Bromwyn swallowed thickly. Her mother *never* spoke of her lost

Way of the Heart.

Jessamin looked down at her hands, which shook more than usual. "You do not know how devastating love can be. When you love someone, you give up part of your soul."

"Forgive me," Bromwyn whispered, "I did not mean—"

"Of course you 'did not mean,'" her mother spat, glaring at her daughter. "You never *mean*. You speak your mind before you think your words through. You stab with your tongue, and when you cause pain, you offer your apologies as you watch the blood flow. Well, I am done with this."

Jessamin stood, smoothing the wrinkles from her woolen dress. She lifted her chin high, and the numerous thin braids of her short black hair brushed her shoulders. Tall as Bromwyn was for her age, Jessamin was taller, and she stared down her nose at her daughter. "You think that being in love with the one you marry would make any difference? Life is cruel, Daughter. And fate is crueler still."

"I am sorry," Bromwyn said, her voice small and full of sorrow.

Jessamin took a shaky breath. "I know. In time, I will forgive you. But not now. Not yet."

Bromwyn bowed her head, forcing her tears to stay within her eyes. She would not cry. As much as she hated disappointing her grandmother, which seemed to be a daily occurrence, disappointing her mother was far worse. She loved her mother, and yet she lashed out at Jessamin more and more, for reasons she didn't understand.

*Why am I full of such rage?* Bromwyn swallowed, desperately trying to remain calm, impassive, in the way that was expected of witches.

33

*Why do I hurt someone I love, and so easily?*

*Why am I so inhuman?*

"I must prepare for my readings," her mother said coldly. "And you must perform your studies." She sniffed. "It is quite obvious that even with your grandmother's curse upon you, you still do not master your emotions. And unless that happens, you will not pass your test."

Bromwyn bit her lip. She didn't know which caused her more distress: her upcoming marriage or her dreaded test of Witchcraft. Bromwyn had no idea what her test would actually be, let alone when it would occur; whatever the test was, it would happen sometime during her apprenticeship. Neither her mother nor her grandmother would speak of it, other than to tell her it would be soon, and that Bromwyn would have only one chance to pass. If she failed, she would have to cut her hair and lose her magic.

Like her mother.

"Go," Jessamin said. "You may not have lessons with your grandmother today, but between your studies and your errands, you have much to fill your time. You will be stopping by the forge, yes?"

Not trusting her voice, Bromwyn nodded.

"Good. Do give Brend my regards."

With that, Jessamin parted the curtain that separated Bromwyn's bedroom from the front of the shop and walked out.

Bromwyn stared at the cascading fabric, which once again fell into place, dividing mother from daughter. With a heavy sigh, she began to shrug out of her wedding gown.

# FAR FROM COMFORTABLE

The sun glared at Bromwyn as she strode down the main avenue of Loren. She felt the heat on her head and back, but she did not sweat. One of the first things Bromwyn had taught herself (quietly, of course; her grandmother was a firm believer in not experimenting with magic until you were old enough to undo the damage you would undoubtedly cause, so much of Bromwyn's early years as a witch had been spent working the fun part of magic on the sly) was to spell her clothing to keep her body cool in the summer and warm in the winter. So she walked now, her thick black hair curling down to her knees, her dress heavy and proper, her feet bare, and though the sun did its best to have her bake in her garments, Bromwyn was untouched by the heat.

She knew such comfort was merely an illusion, for her Way was of Sight, and so she could not actually prevent herself from feeling the weather's touch. Her comfort was a lie. Even so, she was happy to believe in that lie, if it meant not sweating through her dress.

Walking the Loren streets this summer morning, Bromwyn was not alone. But none of the passersby engaged her in conversation other than the barest whisper of a "Good morning." She pretended, as always, that it did not sting. So she walked with her chin high and kept her mouth fixed in a smile. It was the polite thing to do, especially considering that one day she would be the Wise One of Loren. The villagers grudgingly had learned to accept her—and never mind that until she had become apprenticed at the age of ten to her grandmother, they had happily acknowledged her as the cartomancer's daughter—but the people of Loren were far from comfortable with her. At least they didn't outright fear her, as they did her grandmother.

Then again, everyone was afraid of Niove Whitehair.

Bromwyn walked, and around her, Loren thrived in the way that villages did. The sounds of daily life rang out: the bustle of people talking and walking, of pigs squealing, of dogs barking and carthorses clomping. She ignored them all, just as she ignored the ever-present mud and clutter and the stench of manure piles. Background noise; background smells. Bromwyn had too much on her mind to be bothered by such mundane things.

She crossed the great circle at Loren's center, keeping her gaze straight ahead, as she always did, instead of glancing down the street that led a winding path to the large church. No matter how kind-hearted the village priest was—and indeed, he was a gentle soul who always had a good word for Bromwyn—she would never set foot inside that place of hollow worship, not even on her wedding day. Those who practiced magic and were connected to Nature made all vows outdoors. Even though Bromwyn did not want to marry Brend, she would take her oath of wedlock seriously, as she would for any promise made in her name. That meant she would wed beneath the stars with the moon bearing witness, no matter how much her betrothed might insist otherwise. And whether any god chose to listen to their wedding vows was no business of Bromwyn's.

Wind blew around her, hot and restless, as if in anticipation of the afternoon's Midsummer Festival. *Silly stuff*, Bromwyn thought, for true Midsummer was not until that night, at sunset. But those who did not work with magic tended to observe celebrations in the daylight.

And now that Bromwyn thought about it, it was safer for the common folk to do exactly that. They considered the fey to be nothing more than storybook fairies, tales to delight their children and to frighten them into behaving "lest the boggies get them," as many Loren parents threatened—which was pure foolishness, because all the ballybogs would do if they caught human children was get them filthy from head to foot, which Bromwyn suspected most children would thoroughly enjoy.

If the villagers knew just how dangerous most of the fey truly were, and how close Loren was to one of the World Doors that connected to the magical land of the fey, she suspected there would be a mass exodus that would leave the village husked out, barren. So even though it frustrated her, she allowed the

37

people of Loren their illusion of safety.

Being a Wise One, her grandmother often said, meant knowing when to remain silent.

Around her, the breeze picked up strength. The wind carried with it the smells and sounds of Loren, and Bromwyn closed her eyes as she breathed deeply, pushing aside her uneasy thoughts and wrapping herself in the scents of life. Over the underlying smell of the village itself—stone and earth and wood and refuse, their odors blending and tickling in the back of her throat—she caught the tantalizing aromas of cinnamon and sugar. And then her mouth began to water.

She hurried over to her favorite shop, and she paused there, hoping for a whiff of apple pie or, better yet, sugar cookies. Jessamin was a fine cook, and Bromwyn herself was no stranger to the ways of the kitchen, for food carried its own sort of magic. But neither of them could hold a candle to Mistress Baker and her renowned pastries.

People crowded inside the bakery and loitered outside, waiting for their morning breads and other such foods. Bromwyn knew that because today (well, tonight) was Midsummer, customers would purchase more than usual, both for the afternoon celebration in the Village Circle and for the ritual of leaving fresh bread, ripe fruit, and clotted cream on their doorsteps for their storybook fairies to take at night. Bromwyn wondered, as she glanced at the rows filled with cooling pies, why the villagers bothered with such meaningless gestures; they must have suspected that vermin ate the bread and berries, and stray cats took the cream. To the good people of Loren, Midsummer seemed nothing more than an excuse to be festive and waste food.

Bromwyn knew that the true reason for Midsummer Festival was to entertain the fey on their annual visit to the land. And that enjoyment had nothing to do with bread or berries or milk. Their hunger was for something else entirely.

*Enough*, she told herself. She shouldn't be thinking dark thoughts on such a bright morning.

Bromwyn peeked inside the baker's door, looking for a glimpse of red hair. But no—if Rusty was in the shop at all, he was out of her view. If anything, he was probably running ingredients from the basement storehouse to the ovens in the back, judging by the line of customers waiting their turn. Bromwyn smiled as she imagined Rusty covered in enough powdered sugar to turn his hair pink.

As she walked past the bakery, she felt a soft nudge against her back.

Her hand whipped out behind her, and she grabbed hold. There was a yelp as she yanked her arm forward, and now in front of her was a mudrat of a child, whom she held by one skinny arm.

He blinked wide brown eyes at her, looking like quite the waif as he obviously prepared to give her a sad tale of parents lost and an empty belly forcing him to steal. Then something passed over his dirty face, and his eyes became glassy with fear.

"Lady Witch," he stuttered. "I'm sorry! I didn't know it was you! I swear it!"

She released him, but he stood rooted to the spot. Maybe one day, she would appreciate people's fear of her, as her grandmother insisted again and again. But right now, all it did was make her feel tired, and uneasy, and very much the monster.

"Usually the long hair is a dead giveaway," she said with a smile that she hoped was soothing.

But the child paled, and she realized her mistake. She could have kicked herself for the poor choice of words.

"I," he said. "I. I."

"You," she prodded gently.

"I'm sorry! I didn't mean! Here!" He thrust something at her—a small roll of bread, probably snatched just moments ago from one of the bakery shelves.

"Please," she said, "this is not necessary … "

"Take it," he shrieked, dropping it into her hand.

She closed her fingers around the roll and he took off, fleeing down the dirt-packed street and rounding a corner that would eventually lead toward the docks, as if he could outrun her magic had she chosen to lay a curse on him.

She sighed. Stupid mudrat.

Breaking off a small piece of the roll, she popped the morsel into her mouth. The bread was indeed fresh, and still warm, and she enjoyed the snack as she walked on. As she chewed, she thought about turning back toward the bakery to say hello to Rusty.

She smiled wryly. Had she seen him, he would have made a joke about her bare feet, or about how he was thinner than she was, or about her hair being so long that it was practically a dress. Rusty always teased her. If it were anyone else saying such things to her, Bromwyn would have gotten angry—not that the others in the village treated her like an ordinary girl, but if they had, she was certain she would have scolded them until her tongue bled. But with Rusty, she didn't get angry. Instead, she teased back. True, there were times when she threatened to turn him into a toad, but that was only when he was being particularly thickheaded. He couldn't help himself; after all, he was a boy.

Lost in thoughts of the red-haired apprentice baker, Bromwyn also lost track of where she was until a clanging sound jostled her. She blinked, and her nostrils flared. The reek of charcoal overwhelmed the scent of fresh bread, and when she swallowed the last bite of her roll, the food tasted faintly of ashes.

She had arrived at the forge.

There stood Brend, soot-covered and sweaty, forcing metal to his will as he hammered some weapon or other against an anvil. He had eschewed his shirt, as usual, and beneath the leather apron that covered his chest, his muscles bulged. Brend was a strong man of eighteen, and Bromwyn had no doubt that he would become even stronger as he grew older. He cut an imposing figure, and if she had truly been concerned about her own protection, then she would have looked no further than Brend Underhill, apprentice of Nick Ironside.

But she did not want protection. She wanted love, eventually. For now, she wanted freedom.

No matter; she was not to have either.

The familiar bitterness welled up in her belly, and she forced it down. Brend had been one of the village children she had grown up with, all of them playing together and filling the streets with shouts of laughter. But once she had become apprenticed to her grandmother, those children, including Brend, looked the other way when she would walk by. Out of all of them, only Rusty had remained true; only Rusty still laughed with her and teased, not caring that she was a witch who could spell him into a toad.

Out of all of them, Brend had been the first to walk away.

At the age of ten, Bromwyn had learned how easy it was to be hurt by those she cared about, and how quickly friends could become strangers.

But none of that mattered now. Standing in the doorway of the forge, her eyes already watering from the charcoal dust riding the air, Bromwyn stretched her mouth into a proper smile. Perhaps this morning, Brend would be civil. Most of the villagers let their grudges and prejudices pass on a festival day, and today (well, tonight) was Midsummer.

Nostrils crisping from the fumes and the heat, she called out, "Good morning, Sir Smith."

Brend stiffened, then glanced over his shoulder to regard her. At least now he met her dark gaze; when they had first been betrothed a year ago, he had barely been able to glance in her direction. Either he had grown bolder regarding her, or he simply was too busy to bother with showing his unease around her. Bromwyn didn't mind either possibility. Anything was better than being feared by the one she was supposed to marry.

Her stomach pitched from the thought of her upcoming wedding, and she ground her teeth together to keep smiling.

After an indeterminable amount of time passed, he acknowledged her and said, "Lady Witch." As always, his tone was proper, and cold, and completely out of place with the heat of the hearth fire in its pit. He gripped his hammer tight enough to whiten his knuckles, and the set of his shoulders showed he was ready for violence. Beneath him, his anvil gleamed as it caught the firelight. Voice tight, Brend asked, "What brings you to the forge this morning?"

Bromwyn kept her smile in place. "As every morning, I simply wished to see you and bid you a good day."

"Lady Witch is too kind."

"My mother sends her regards."

"Do extend my thanks."

"She thinks highly of your master," Bromwyn said, grasping for conversation. And it was true; Jessamin always spoke fondly of Old Nick, praising his strong arm and stoic character. That was why, she had said many a time over the past year, Jessamin had matched her daughter with his apprentice.

There was a pause, as heavy as the dusty air. Bromwyn had reached the limit of small talk; anything further would be prying.

Fire and Air, why did the man have to make this so difficult?

She asked, "Where is Master Smith this morning? Surely not preparing for Midsummer." The thought of the village blacksmith taking part in the afternoon's festivities was enough to make her lips twitch in a sudden smile. Old Nick was not one to do anything even remotely considered fun. He was like her grandmother in that regard.

"Off to the smelter's for iron."

She floundered for conversation. "And that is not something for the apprentice?"

His eyes punched a hole through her. "What Master Smith deems appropriate for his apprentice is surely no concern of yours."

She felt a blush smack her face, the embarrassment more brutal than the forge's heat. "I meant no disrespect. I was only curious."

"It's not your business," he said abruptly, thrusting his tools into a vat of liquid. Over the hiss, he said, "As I don't ask you about your deviltry, so you won't ask me about my work."

"Deviltry?" she echoed, stunned. "Surely you joke."

He scowled at her. "Magic isn't natural."

Perhaps her curse had come into effect this morning after all; how else to explain that just after her mother had warned her of small-minded people thinking foolishness about witches, her own bridegroom turned out to be one of those fools?

"Magic is more natural than blending metals at inhuman temperatures," she said, her voice rising, "more natural than forcing iron to your will. I never force Nature to do anything, unlike you with your hammer!"

Sparks crackled in the fire pit as the two betrothed glared at each other.

"This is a mockery," she said at last. "Will you not speak with your mother? Why should we be thrust into a marriage neither of us wants?"

He growled, "A son does what his parents ask. Maybe a witch doesn't bother with such things."

"Our differences are too great," she said through clenched teeth. "It cannot work."

He shrugged, an easy roll of his massive shoulders, but his expression belied the movement. "We have no say in the matter."

She wanted to scream, to grab his hammer and hurl it against the wall. But he was right: They had no say. They were trapped by the decisions of others. The unfairness of it ate at her heart.

Bromwyn managed a curtsey. "Until tomorrow, Sir Smith."

He nodded, once, and then he showed her his back. It was broad, and peppered with fire scars, and unforgiving.

She fled.

Only when she was atop her mother's shop, safe on the wooden roof and away from nervous stares and critical gazes did she allow herself to cry, briefly and silently. Then she called herself three kinds of fool, wiped away her tears, and began to practice her spells. The first attempt fizzled and died before it left her fingertips. The second fared little better. But the third took hold, and magic sparkled as she worked through the movements.

After an hour, all that existed was Bromwyn and her magic; nothing else mattered. She was focused. Determined. She would master her emotions, even if she had to turn her heart into stone to do so.

# THE BAKER'S SON

"Good Midsummer to you, Winnie!"

Bromwyn flinched, and then she bit her lip as her spell slipped away from her control. "Fire and Air," she muttered as she tried to recast the magic before the pain began. Ignoring Rusty—who'd bounded over the rooftop, she had no doubt, like some storybook hero—she slowly coaxed the spell back into proper form. Sitting cross-legged, her hands resting lightly on her lap, she appeared to be relaxed; only the sweat beading on her brow showed her effort.

"Winnie? Don't you hear me?"

*A deaf mule would hear you,* she thought with a scowl—and then the entire casting crumbled. Bromwyn didn't have the chance to direct the power from the broken spell before it slammed into her, and she gasped as wild magic surged through her until it felt like her skin was aflame. With a hiss, she channeled the energy into the air, where it crackled and sparked like heat lightning.

After what felt like an eternity of burning alive, the pain subsided. Bromwyn sighed in relief. The she glowered. By Nature's grace, she hated losing control of her magic! It made her feel like a child, to say nothing of the physical pain. Oh, her grandmother would have such words with her if she knew that Bromwyn's concentration could slip when she cast even a basic spell. And Niove used her hands a lot during such conversations.

A bleak thought wormed its way into her mind: What if she could not cast properly during her test?

She took a deep breath and told herself not to panic. She had been studying the Ways of Witchcraft for nearly seven years. She would pass her test, and she would keep her magic. There was nothing else for it; without magic, Bromwyn was nothing. And she was too stubborn to ever be reduced to nothing.

Behind her, Rusty snorted. "No answer, Lady Witch? Truly, my feelings are hurt."

She looked over her shoulder. There he stood, looking proud as a storybook peacock, and no matter that he was a beanpole of a boy in ill-fitting clothing, with a floppy brown hat that completely covered his auburn hair: Derek Jonasson, called Rusty, apprentice baker of Loren. Whenever she called him Sir Baker, he threatened to box her ears.

"A good morning to you, Rusty," she said brightly, pushing aside her nerves over her upcoming test. "You know as well as I that your feelings are well protected by your infallible ego, so do not play the rogue with me. And true Midsummer is not until tonight."

Rusty placed his hands over his chest. "Wounded to the soul!" he cried, and then he collapsed to the ground. His wide-brimmed hat fell over his face.

She giggled. "Your soul is equally protected by your ego, silly boy."

"Boy?" Rusty stretched his legs long, and then he sprang to his feet with the grace of an acrobat. Standing tall, he plucked his hat from mid-air and placed it rakishly on his head. "I'm no more a boy than you are a girl."

"I am sixteen," she said with a shrug. "Village law clearly brands me a child until my seventeenth birthday."

"You're old enough to be married to hulking Brend come autumn."

"When I will be seventeen."

"If you're old enough to be almost married, then you're a woman," Rusty insisted. "And as I'm a full thirty days your senior, that makes me a man. Boy, indeed!" He harrumphed, and ruined the effect with a laugh. "'Boyish charm.' Yes, you meant to say 'boyish charm.' Apology accepted!"

Bromwyn muffled another giggle. "As you say."

"Indeed I do. Say, I didn't mean to interrupt your witchy thing."

She smiled fondly. *Witchy thing.* Those who didn't cast magic couldn't possibly understand the concentration it took, or how draining it was. At least he wasn't awed by her power. To him, she was Winnie. Had anyone else attempted to call her by such an endearment, she would have spelled the offender's clothing with imaginary fire ants.

"It was of no consequence," she said. "Ending my practice early will harm me none."

"Glad to hear it," he said, extending a hand to her. "Magic makes me itch."

Bromwyn placed her hand in his, allowing him to help her to her feet. "That would be all of the flour that found its way into your shirt. How did you escape the bakery, today of all days?"

He grinned hugely. "You're assuming I was there in the first place."

She groaned. "Rusty ... "

"Don't you 'Rusty' me," he said, wagging a finger at her. "I've had years and years of Midsummer Festival baking misery, and when I got up before dawn today to start hauling sacks of flour, I decided I've had quite enough of it, thank you. Besides, I'm sure my da is happy I'm not there. I accidentally burned the bread yesterday."

"An accident, eh?"

"Truth," he swore emphatically. "It stank up the shop something fierce. Customers walked out. Da was furious."

Bromwyn thought of how she had so easily infuriated Jessamin earlier. "As you with your father yesterday, so was I with my mother today."

"You burned the bread in your mam's kitchen?"

"I said things I should never have voiced." She let out a tired sigh. "It seems that both of us have been grave disappointments as of late."

Rusty grabbed her hands and began to dance with her across the roof, ignoring her startled protest.

"My darling Winnie," he crowed, "you're far too serious for me!"

"I am *supposed* to be serious!" she screeched. "I am a witch!"

"So?" he asked as he dipped her. "When did you trade your sense of humor for magic?"

"Let me go!"

"Now? As I'm dipping you? Seems dangerous, if you ask me."

"Rusty!" she spluttered. "Fire and Air, let me up! Now! Or I shall magic you into a toad!"

"That's how it is, then?" He pulled her back up and continued to lead her in a dance. "Threatening poor villagers who don't grasp your magical know-how?"

She twisted out of his arms and fumed at him as he continued waltzing. *Be calm*, she commanded herself. *Do. Not. Get. Angry.*

She growled, "You make me forget myself."

"Like that's so hard."

Her look should have killed him on the spot. "Rusty!"

"Tell me, Winnie," he said as he danced, "what has your garters in a knot this fine morn? It has to be more than you and your mam pecking at each other like hens."

Bromwyn took a deep breath and stilled herself to calmness. "I did poorly at my practice today. I must focus more, and keep better control of my temper." Her voice raised a notch. "Which is difficult to do when you dance me across my mother's rooftop."

"So you are not allowing yourself to have any fun, eh? Fine then. I've just the thing to cheer you up. After my dance is done, I'll show you what I've nicked."

She frowned deeply at him. "You are still playing at being a thief?"

"Not playing, my darling," he said as he turned. "I *am* a thief. A damn good one, too, I'm happy to say."

"You are a lucky boy, but only a mediocre thief. It will cause you trouble."

Rusty looked appalled as he bowed. "What?"

"I said—"

"Who're you calling a boy?"

"You." With a wicked grin, she darted behind him and kicked him lightly in the rump. "*Boy.*"

Off-balance, Rusty tottered. He pin-wheeled his arms, turned his sprawl into a cartwheel, and landed squarely on his feet.

"Masterful control of your temper, Lady Witch," he said, picking up his hat.

"That was not temper," she sniffed. "That was to emphasize my point."

"What sort of point are you trying to make?"

"That you are a fool. Thieves get caught, Rusty."

"Only the bad ones."

"Exactly why I am worried about you."

"Oh," he said, clutching his chest, "the pain!"

She let her glare speak for her.

"No need for your worry, I'm happy to say. I'm a good thief." He grinned at her, a lovely, lopsided grin, and it tried to chip away at the stone around her heart.

She lifted her chin as if that could deflect his charm. "So you say."

"And so I am. I'll be more than a baker's son, and if that means I have to steal my way to do it, so be it."

By Nature's grace, he could be such a *boy!* "If you would only *work* for it, it would not seem such a stretch!"

"Spoken like someone who's never broken her back hauling sacks or burned her hands when scouring ovens." His grin remained, but it hardened until it looked brittle enough to break. "Don't tell me how to live my life, Bromwyn Darkeyes. I don't tell you how to live yours. I'm a thief, and I'm proud of it."

She crossed her arms over her chest and scowled at him. Fire and Air, he was such an idiot! Did he not see the danger of flouncing about and picking pockets? How could he be blind to the ugly truths about thievery? Everyone knew that thieves, once caught, met the business end of a chopping block. If they were lucky, they lost only a hand.

Then again, Rusty was a lucky boy. At the very least, he had been lucky so far.

He let out a strained laugh. "Look at us, arguing about the way I spend my time. We sound like my folks. Good practice for when you marry Brend, eh?"

She tried to smile—she really did.

"Peace, Winnie," he said, laughing for real this time. "You have too beautiful a face to ruin it with that scowl of yours. Here, this'll make everything right as rain." He reached into his pocket and pulled out a small silver marble. "I was going to give this to Jalsa, but it's yours if you want it."

Something gripped her heart and squeezed. "So you are still mooning over the serving girl?" she asked lightly.

"She's no girl," he said, his voice dreamy.

Bromwyn rolled her eyes. "So you are still mooning over the serving *woman?*"

"You're a woman, Winnie. But she's a wench. And yes, I'm still mooning over her." He sighed happily. "Same as most every man in Loren, not to mention five villages over. Poets worship Jalsa's face. Minstrels worship Jalsa's eyes. Dockworkers worship Jalsa's—"

"So," Bromwyn said, her knife-like smile neatly cutting off his voice, "a silver marble. How..." She struggled to find the word. "Unique."

"Real beaut, eh? Figure it's got to be worth at least ten silver. But if you want it, it's yours. It could be your good luck charm!" He dropped it into her hand.

As soon as the cool orb touched her palm, her skin began to tingle.

Her voice tight, she asked, "You bought this?"

"Why would I spend good money when things are there for the taking?" Rusty chuckled. "I relieved it from a crone so daft, she's still combing her chin whiskers instead of knowing I've nicked her."

"This has been spelled," Bromwyn gritted. She stared at Rusty until he squirmed. "There is a powerful illusion on this."

Rusty frowned. "You certain?"

"Yes." Her Way of Sight meant that she easily saw when illusions had been placed.

"Now that's just unfair."

"Says the boy who steals." She could almost see the true shape beneath the marble. Bromwyn touched it with her magic, but the ball resisted. Interesting—there was a ward around the illusion. This was no basic spell. She asked, "From whom did you take this?"

Rusty scratched his head. "She was an old lady, Winnie. Bent over, wrapped in a shawl. Like all old ladies, you know?"

And then she saw what lay beneath the magic, and she felt ice creep up her spine.

She hissed, "As I live and breathe, Rusty, you are the biggest fool I know!"

"She was an old woman, Win. What's the danger?"

"You want to know what the danger is?" She jabbed a finger at his chest. "You stole this from my *grandmother*."

Rusty went very pale. "Oh." Then his legs buckled and he sat on the ground, hard. "Damn me."

# A STOLEN KEY

Bromwyn paced. "Now, the fact that you are still alive is troublesome. She should have stricken you down by now."

"I didn't know," Rusty moaned. "I swear, I didn't know!"

She paused to glare at him. "And what difference do you think that will make?"

"But," Rusty stammered, "maybe she doesn't know yet."

"She knows. She knows almost everything." Actually, Bromwyn was certain that her grandmother knew everything, always. But she didn't want Rusty's heart to stop out of fright. She began pacing again. "So you are not dead, which is a good thing. That means she wanted you to take the Key." She froze. "That makes no sense. Why would she want that? It is *her* Key. She cannot just … just … *give* it away. That would be madness!"

"Key?" he asked weakly.

She blinked at him, her thoughts still whirling over the possibility—no, the probability—that her grandmother had just foisted one of the most important objects in all the realms to a boy thief with no sense of responsibility.

"Key," she repeated. "I will remove the illusion. Hold out your hand."

He did so, and Bromwyn dropped the marble into his open palm. Then she focused on the small orb and, murmuring words of power, she slowly began to peel away the layers of spelled light. First, the color corrected itself, dulling from a winking silver to a stormy gray, and then the shape lengthened and flattened until it finally settled into its true form: an iron key.

Once the spell was removed, Bromwyn swayed and closed her eyes. Her head throbbed, and she held her breath as she pushed her dizziness aside. Her grandmother's strengths were in Ways other than Sight, so when Niove would cast an illusion, she tended to overcompensate.

A hand on her shoulder steadied her. Bromwyn opened her eyes to see Rusty looking sickly at her, his grin more like a silent scream.

He asked, "You feeling all right, Win?"

"Yes," she replied. "It was a strong spell. Casting enough magic to unravel it drained me. I will be fine, thank you."

"Good."

She quirked an eyebrow. "Worried?"

Rusty nodded.

A smile flitted across her lips, one that she quashed

immediately. Of course Rusty had been concerned for her welfare; they were friends, and friends cared about each other. She should not feel ... flattered ... over such a thing. Emotions, she decided, were just stuff and nonsense—they interfered when casting spells, and they interfered when *not* casting spells.

Then Rusty said, "Bad enough I've stolen from your granny. Worse would be if you passed out, and I had to fetch her to make you better." He shuddered.

Bromwyn narrowed her eyes. "As you can see," she said coolly, "your fear was misplaced."

"I'll be sure to keep it somewhere safe for next time." He stared at the Key. "So. An iron key. What does it unlock?" He perked up. "A treasure chest, maybe?"

"No," she growled, "not a treasure chest. And it unlocks nothing. Its purpose is only to lock." She pushed away from him and began pacing again, wondering whether her grandmother was insane.

After a time, Rusty cleared his throat. "Bromwyn, my darling, you're pacing. That means you're nervous. Shouldn't *I* be the one fretting right about now? I'm the one who nicked from your granny. And from what you've said many a time, she's got no sense of humor."

Bromwyn halted and looked at Rusty, who even now was grinning a little more naturally, his eyes sparkling with mirth. He probably thought this was grand, like something out of a storybook. The thief who had stolen from a powerful witch! Now all he needed was an angry dragon, and a pile of gold, and a fair maiden to rescue—then he'd be quite the hero!

Rage coursed through her, causing her limbs to tremble. "Yes," she replied, "you should be fretting. Tonight is Midsummer."

"So?"

Through clenched teeth, she said, "Every Midsummer, my grandmother must greet the fey as they enter our world. She is their Guardian, the one who welcomes them to our land for the one night each year they are permitted to visit." She forced her anger down, and when she next spoke, her tone was measured and flat. "More important than that, the Guardian is the one who makes sure that the fey follow the rules of conduct. And most important of all, the Guardian locks the World Door behind the fey when they leave at dawn."

"Fey." Beneath his wide-brimmed hat, Rusty's brow creased. "That's fairies, right?"

"Indeed."

"So fairies are real?"

"Very."

"But aren't they tiny things? Pixies and elves and such?"

"They come in all sizes," she said. "But the tiny ones tend to have the biggest appetite for human flesh."

He blinked at her. "Really?"

"Really."

"Oh," he said, paling. "That's not in the stories ... "

"No." Bromwyn once again paced along the length of her mother's rooftop. "But their penchant for stealing human children *is* in the stories. That and their preferred food are two of the reasons why there have to be rules in place. And that is why there has to be a Guardian."

"The stories seem to leave out lots of things," Rusty said uneasily.

"Oh, yes," Bromwyn agreed. "They speak of the Midsummer Festival and all the dancing and music that the fey enjoy, but they do not mention Guardians at all, or what the consequences would be if a Guardian fails."

"I don't want to know this, do I?"

Bromwyn sniffed at him. "Yes, you do. If a Guardian fails, the fey would be free to return every night for a year, and wreak havoc among the mortals."

"See, now that I know about." Rusty's voice took on a note of excitement. "Spoiling milk, nicking strawberries, knocking over furniture ... "

"Stealing children and eating their parents ... "

"Oh," Rusty said, deflating. "Right. I guess they do that in between all of the music and dancing and such."

"Having the fey walk among the mortals night after night would be 'akin to setting a fox inside a henhouse,'" Bromwyn said, quoting from one of her mother's tomes on the fey. "So the Guardian must be diligent and watchful and very strict. And powerful, of course, lest the fey challenge the Guardian for the right to walk the land every night instead of just during Midsummer."

"Sounds like being the Guardian is no fun at all," Rusty said. "And rather daunting. So it's perfect for your gran."

She nodded. "She is a very good Guardian. I once heard that the fey King and Queen consider her a peer." For a moment, Bromwyn remembered a flaxen-haired pixie with piercingly blue eyes and a wicked grin. Then she pushed that memory away. "All of the fey respect my grandmother."

"As well they should."

Bromwyn shot Rusty a look. "No need to practice your flattery on me when it is meant for others."

He held up his hands. "Sorry, sorry, sorry."

She glared at him for a moment longer, allowing herself to feel her anger and her frustration, then she tamped those feelings down and continued her bristling pace. She said, "As long as I have lived, my grandmother has been the Guardian. But the rule is that the one who holds the Key is the Guardian."

There was a pause, filled with the sounds of Bromwyn's bare feet slapping the rooftop as she marched.

Rusty said, "Now that's a stupid rule."

"There are always rules, especially when it comes to magic and the fey."

He harrumphed. "Inconvenient! Who created all these rules?"

"Witches' rules of magic have been in place for thousands of years," she said. "They were set to ensure that those who follow a Way of Witchcraft do not use so much of Nature's power that they burn themselves out. The rules concerning the fey, however, were created by the fey themselves."

"What? Why?"

"Out of boredom, I suppose."

"That's completely ridiculous."

"They do not die," she said, shrugging, "and for some of them, their power is almost limitless. I imagine that it is more fun to play games when you have to work your way around limitations rather than simply getting what you want whenever you want it."

Rusty snorted. "If *I* were one of these fey, I'd be quite content with getting what I wanted all the time. I'd be happy to show them what they're missing."

"Do not joke about the fey," she said sharply, halting in front of him. "Once you joke, it is easy to forget how dangerous they are, let alone how much trouble you are in. Thanks to your pick pocketing, you hold the Key. You are the Guardian. And tonight is Midsummer."

Rusty was silent as he considered her words.

"Well," he finally said, I don't suppose your granny would be willing to just take the Key back, would she?"

Now there was an idea. "One way to find out."

"I snuck away from the bakery only to run to the Wise One. This day isn't going as I'd planned." Rusty let out a mournful sigh. "I'm really in trouble, aren't I?"

"Yes, you really are." Bromwyn met his eyes. "But maybe my grandmother is in a forgiving mood today."

"Likely?" Rusty asked as they started toward the door that led down to her mother's shop.

"No," Bromwyn admitted. Then she opened the door and let Rusty through, and she wondered how she could convince her grandmother to take back the Key.

# A NOTE

Rusty was huffing and puffing by the time they reached the outskirts of the Allenswood.

"Damn me," he wheezed, "why couldn't you just magic us there?"

"That skill is beyond me," Bromwyn said, not even breathing hard. "But even if I could, you would probably become nauseated should I have done so. Coaxing Nature to do something so extreme tends to unsettle the stomach."

"My stomach is unsettled already. The whole idea of me being this fairy Guardian is enough to make me lose my breakfast."

"Poor boy. At least the walk is helping to settle your tender belly."

"It's doing no such thing."

"And it has given me time to think of how to approach

Grandmother. Now stop complaining and put on your charming face. We are almost there."

Rusty let out a beleaguered sigh, but he kept pace with her.

Bromwyn walked lightly, and despite the severity of Rusty's situation, she couldn't help but enjoy the feeling of the earth and grass under her bare feet (which were so filthy that they would have given her mother a case of the nerves). With every step, she felt the hum of the world pulsing beneath her, like a heartbeat buried deep within the land itself. And it brought a smile to her lips.

This was why she hated wearing shoes: Barefoot, she was connected to Nature. The few times she had to coax her feet into boots—when the snows came, for instance, or when the dirt roads were transformed to mud by the heavy spring rains—she felt half blind. When she was younger, she had asked her grandmother how she could stand to cover her feet every day. Niove had answered with a question of her own: "How can you stand the feeling of sharp rocks biting your heels, or baked dirt scalding your toes?" When Bromwyn had shrugged and said, "I just do," her grandmother replied, "And there is your answer."

Bromwyn had discovered at a young age that getting straight answers from her grandmother was rarely as simple as a "yes" or a "no."

They walked on, and soon Rusty wrapped his arms around himself and shivered. "Did it just get cold?"

She nodded. "We just crossed the threshold onto my grandmother's land."

"I never get cold like this in your mam's shop."

"My mother is not a witch," Bromwyn said abruptly. "And both the shop and our residence are hers, not mine. There is no magical threshold there."

He rubbed his arms. "So it's cold like this every time you visit your gran? Not exactly welcoming, is it?"

"Visit?" Bromwyn echoed. "The last time I *visited* my grandmother was just before I became her apprentice. I do not *visit* her. I work with her almost daily, and I have a bedroom there for those times when it is too late for me to travel back to the village."

Rusty grinned. "So snippety, Lady Witch. And all because I asked a question. Which, by the way, you didn't answer."

She glared at him. "I was not being 'snippety.'"

"You were too. And still being evasive with the answers, I see."

Bromwyn narrowed her eyes, but all that did was make Rusty grin wider. So she sighed, and she reminded herself of her temper. "I feel a change as I cross her threshold, but it does not seem cold to me. More like there is a thickness in the air that I pass through."

"Do all witches have these threshold things around their places?"

"Yes."

He slid her an odd look that she could not interpret. "So when you and Brend marry, will I get cold whenever I walk past the smithy?"

His words sent spikes of fire up her spine. "The forge is Nick Ironside's," she said, walking faster. "It does not belong to Brend. And it will never be mine."

Huffing to keep up, Rusty asked, "What about your house, then? Surely you won't be living over the smithy, what with all the dust and the heat and the stink."

"One hopes," she muttered. With Brend, who could know? "What about my house?"

"Will it set my teeth a-chatter whenever I think of strolling by?"

"Why?" she asked, unable to keep the bitterness from her voice. "Will you be visiting me in my happy home, when I am Mistress Smith?"

"Not if it means I'll need a winter cloak in the summer."

"The cold is because of Grandmother's Way. Mine is different. The threshold for my home should be more ... " She searched for the proper word. "Warm," she said feebly.

"Good. I don't like the cold." He puffed out a frosty breath, as if to emphasize how chilly the air had become. "Makes the whole idea of paying a visit rather unpleasant."

Bromwyn hadn't thought about actually living with Brend once they said their vows, and now that she turned the idea around in her mind, she was very troubled. Bad enough she was being forced to marry someone she didn't like, let alone love. Worse would be if Brend's mistrust of her magic prevented her from making her magical presence known in their home.

*Well,* she decided grimly, *no matter how he feels about it, I am a witch. I will not hide what I am just to appease his ignorance. Deviltry, indeed!*

They walked the rest of the way in silence. Perhaps Rusty tried to engage her in conversation, but Bromwyn was so lost in thought that nothing short of a shout would have snagged her attention. In her mind, she was setting up shop as the Wise One of Loren right in her home, no matter what Brend thought of it. Even just imagining his bluster, she seethed. She had no doubt that her thickheaded husband would nail a horseshoe over their dwelling in an attempt to keep her dread power in check! Well, let him find out that such trappings were useless against a witch's magic!

As they approached Niove's cottage, Bromwyn's chest seemed to tighten, and butterflies fluttered in her belly. Thoughts of Brend vanished as she swallowed thickly, and she was surprised by the metallic taste on her tongue. She was scared, she realized with a start.

And not for herself.

She glanced at Rusty, who was rubbing his arms and looking far too pale. But beneath his ridiculous wide-brimmed hat, his eyes sparkled with a manic glee, and his grin stretched from ear to ear. He was scared, like her, but he was also eager. The whole thing was an adventure to him; of that, Bromwyn had no doubt. He probably thought he could sweet-talk her grandmother into taking back the Key, and then he'd even steal a kiss and warm her old heart, and then he and Bromwyn would skip back to the village, laughing the whole way, and then celebrate with fresh sugar cookies from his parents' bakery.

She ground her teeth so hard that sparks should have flown from her mouth. He had no idea how dangerous his situation truly was. Bromwyn shuddered. If Rusty was the Guardian tonight, the fey would eat him alive.

Possibly literally.

Well then, her grandmother had to take back the Key, and that was all there was to it. Bromwyn would convince her if Rusty could not. Should it come down to it, Bromwyn would beg. The very idea left a sour taste in her mouth, but she would do what needed to be done.

Rusty couldn't be the Guardian. That would be horrifically bad, both for Rusty and the entire village of Loren.

With that thought in the forefront of her mind, Bromwyn stepped onto her grandmother's stoop and rapped her knuckles on the wooden door. Had she been arriving for a day of studies, she would have entered through the back door without bothering to knock, but this was a different sort of call. A visit, as Rusty had put it. And so, formality was in order.

As she waited like a stranger on the doorstep, Bromwyn wondered if she should have worn shoes.

After a full minute had passed, Rusty whispered, "Maybe you should knock harder?"

"My grandmother is old, not deaf," she said. But she knocked again, louder.

Once again, there was no answer.

The two friends exchanged a look, and then Bromwyn circled round to the back of the cottage with Rusty fast on her heels. She turned the knob to the back door, and it moved easily in her hand. With a push, the door opened, revealing the large kitchen.

Rusty said, "Your granny's the trusting sort, I see."

"You assume she needs to bother with locks."

"Ah. Good point."

Inside, the kitchen was clean, and dark, and very still. Bromwyn knew this room well, for it was where her grandmother brewed potions and prepared ingredients for magic and meals alike. The wooden countertops displayed various clay bowls and wax candles in their holders, as well as a collection of knives by the small sink. Above one of the counters were open shelves that housed earthenware plates and cups. In one corner of the room, the large pantry doors were closed, hiding the various herbs and flowers that Niove used both for her work and for cooking. In the other corner stood a huge barrel filled with water. A stone fireplace and chimney took up the far wall, with a massive iron cauldron squatting over the blackened fire pit and a small bristle broom to clear away ashes. Overhead, attached by large hooks, hung copper pots of varying sizes. In the center of the kitchen was a wooden table, with four matching chairs.

On the table was a piece of paper, held in place by a smooth stone.

Bromwyn felt her stomach drop to her knees. She stepped into her grandmother's kitchen.

"Winnie?" Rusty called. "Should you be doing that when there's no one home?"

"This from the thief," she muttered as she went straight for the table. She picked up the paper, and as she feared, it was a note addressed to her, written in her grandmother's spidery script.

*Girl,*

*No, I am not here, so you can stop hoping that it will be as simple as you begging me to take back the Key. Gilla from Mooreston needed me to assist her with a problematic birth, so that is where I will be by the time you read this. As I am half a day's journey from you, your thief friend will have to deal with the consequences of his selfish action all by his lonesome.*

*But that will not be the case, will it? No, you will want to help him, because he is your friend and you have a good heart, no matter what some people in this small village may think.*

*Know this: I will not take back the Key. I am done playing Guardian to the fair folk. After three score years of the role, I am all too happy to step aside for younger blood. And I suspect that the fey have become somewhat bored with me. They will be most surprised to see the new Key Bearer—and surprised fey are much less dangerous than bored fey.*

*Tell your friend to use all of the charm of his silver tongue when he speaks with the King and Queen. You should school him in the ways of the fey, and in what to expect. And tell him that the Witch of the Way of Death most humbly suggests that he consider a new pastime. Not all whose pockets he picks will be as lenient as I.*

*As for you, girl, keep your temper. Keep your wits about you even as you curtsey to the fey King and Queen. And keep in mind what they value most. Should you be successful, you will keep your magic.*

*I will be back after the Door has opened tonight. I expect to see things well under control. You are to be the Wise One of Loren. In my absence, you will act the part.*

*N.*

"Fire and Air," Bromwyn whispered.

She did not feel her knees give way—one moment she was standing and reading; the next, she was seated on the floor, hearing her heart beating wildly in her chest, beating the way the fey drums would be beating later that night in the dark of the forest. She thought she heard Rusty calling her name, but she could not answer him.

*And if you succeed, you will keep your magic.*

Her test of Witchcraft was upon her. Here, now.

And she had no idea what she was supposed to do.

# SEEKING HELP

"Winnie? Winnie, what's wrong?"

Bromwyn tried to catch her breath, but it was elusive as smoke. How could *this* be her test? She did not even understand what "this" was—it had been Rusty who had stolen the Key; Rusty, therefore, was the Guardian, not she. So what, exactly, was her test?

"Right, now you're scaring me. Can you hear me?"

She blinked once, and then she turned her head to stare at her friend. Rusty was crouching next to her, waving his hand in front of her eyes.

"Winnie?" His voice sounded small and scared.

"Yes," she said.

He breathed out a "whew," and he grinned at her. "You scared me! You all but fainted, and then you wouldn't answer me. I thought maybe your granny had put a spell on her house against trespassers."

Her grandmother had, in fact, done such a thing—a particularly inventive and nasty spell at that. But Bromwyn saw no reason to mention it to Rusty. Instead she said, "Grandmother left me a note, and it ... startled me."

Rusty plucked it from her numb fingers, and as he read it, his face blanched until he was whiter than the village laundress's fabled sheets. Finally he said, "Damn me," and sat down hard on the floor next to Bromwyn. "This is bad."

"Indeed." Her voice was a bare squeak.

"So I'm stuck babysitting the fairies."

Fire bubbled in her stomach. How could he sound so flippant? So careless? But then, he was careless, wasn't he? Her eyes narrowed as she silently raged at her friend. It was Rusty's carelessness that had gotten him into this situation, his mad desire to steal his way out of his birthright that had put him right here in her grandmother's cottage.

Rusty had done this to himself—but she was tied to it.

"Yes," she snarled. "You are the Guardian. Nature help us all."

He ignored her bluster, which made her want to scream. Eyes on her grandmother's note, he asked, "What's this part about you keeping your magic?"

Her face twisted into a grimace. "None of your concern."

"Now, Winnie—"

"Do not 'Now, Winnie' me!" She glared at him, and somehow she managed to lower her voice. Barely. "You do not study magic.

You know nothing about the Ways of Witchcraft. It is not your concern!" She realized that she was shouting, so she clamped her mouth shut and fumed.

His gaze burned into hers, and she saw unspoken thoughts dancing behind his eyes.

"*You* are my concern, Bromwyn Darkeyes." He snorted and shook his head. "You don't want to tell me, fine. What sort of friend would I be if I didn't at least ask about your witchy things?"

Bromwyn swallowed the lump in her throat. Rusty truly cared about her. He had no casual contempt of her way of life, no easy talk of "deviltry." He was so very different from Brend, from the man she was bound to by a promise she had not made but was required to keep. Brend might protect her, as her mother insisted he would, from threats unknown, but he would never care about her. It would be a loveless marriage, filled only with uneasy stillness and cruel silence.

As if to mock her, Jessamin's words echoed in her mind: *Life is cruel, Daughter. And fate is crueler still.*

She blinked away a sudden rush of tears.

*Stop that!* she scolded herself. *This is not the time, not the place!* Not that it ever would be. She was as trapped in her upcoming marriage as Rusty was in his upcoming role as Guardian.

Turning her head, she dabbed at her eyes.

"Oh ... hey now. Don't go and cry like that."

She felt him put his arm over her shoulders, and now he patted her awkwardly.

"There there, Winnie. It'll be fine. You'll see. Please don't cry."

"I am not crying," she said, angrily blotting her tears. "Witches do not cry."

"No," he said, and she could hear the grin in his voice. "Of course not. Witches also melt in the rain, and they live in candy houses. I've read the stories."

She smiled through her sniffles. "I wish the candy houses part were true."

"But not the melting in the rain?"

"It would make bathing rather inconvenient." She sniffled again. "Thank you. I am all right. Just … feeling overwhelmed."

He squeezed her shoulder. "Completely understandable, as I'm feeling the same way."

They both climbed to their feet, and Bromwyn took the note back from Rusty. As she reread it, her panic returned. Her test, here and now.

Was it as simple as her keeping her temper in check? By Nature's grace, was that it? If she refused to get angry, would that be enough?

No, she realized, for her grandmother specifically mentioned she also had to think clearly while among the fey. Granted, that could be nothing more than good advice all around. But the last part of the note was truly problematic: Bromwyn was supposed to remember "what the fey value most."

As far as she knew, that was a toss-up between human children and human flesh.

She crushed the note in her fist. As ludicrous as it seemed, Rusty playing Guardian was clearly part of her test to be a Wise

One. Should she fail, though, it would be more than just her own magic at stake. If she and Rusty made a wrong move beneath the watchful gaze of the fey King and Queen, the results would be devastating for all of Loren. The fey would return every night for a year—and they would steal away all of the village's children, among other things.

And who could say whether they would limit themselves to one small village?

She pressed her lips together. Rusty couldn't fail. She wouldn't let him.

And she would pass her test, whatever it was. Somehow.

"Come," she said, shoving the crumpled note into the large pocket of her dress. "We have to return to the village."

"For what?"

"To speak to the only other person I know who has had any interaction with the fey."

"Who's that?" He smiled hopefully. "I don't suppose it's Jalsa, by any chance?"

She returned the smile, showing far too many teeth. "Sorry, my boy. We need to speak to my mother." Bromwyn was certain that Jessamin would help them.

* * *

But her mother had other ideas.

"There is nothing I can do," Jessamin insisted.

Her mother sat at her cloth-covered table, ready to smile at anyone who entered her shop. Her cards were laid out in a pattern before her, their vivid colors winking in the candlelight. On a bright day such as today, she didn't need the additional illumination; all the candles really did was make the shop even warmer. But Jessamin swore that her customers expected such trappings when they came to seek their fortune or her advice. Bromwyn thought it was pure foolishness; her mother might as well wear the gaudy shawls and heavy kohl liner of the gypsies if she really wanted to make such an impression. Bromwyn had no patience for such pretense.

She had even less patience for her mother's dismissal. She said, "But you must help him. I have heard Grandmother mention in passing that you have spent time with the fey—"

"As have you, Daughter." Jessamin narrowed her eyes at Bromwyn, and when she spoke again, her voice was sour. "You danced with the King and even refused a gift from him, and you lived to tell the tale. You are more of an expert on such matters than am I."

"That was years and years ago," Bromwyn said angrily. "I do not remember the event properly."

"Such things happen. Memories can be treacherous." Her mother's gaze hardened. "Besides, even if I could help you, I would not. I do not like to think of the fey."

"If you will not help us," Bromwyn implored, her voice low, "then Rusty will fail as Guardian tonight." She darted a glance through the open door. Outside, Rusty was watching one of the mudrats shilling villagers in a shell game. The red-haired boy slouched against her mother's shop wall, his large hat perched over his eyes as if he were dozing, but Bromwyn knew that he was keenly attuned to every move of the street child's hands. Learning. Scheming. Determined to be a thief, no matter what the consequences.

Her mother sniffed and she flipped a card. "That is his problem."

Bromwyn turned to gape at Jessamin. "This is more important than your petty hatreds, Mother!"

"*Petty.*" Jessamin spat the word. "You do not know that of which you speak."

"Of course I do!" Bromwyn said, stomping her foot. "If he fails, all of Loren will suffer! And for what? To appease your wounded pride? To soothe your own hurts of long ago, whatever they were?"

Jessamin slammed her hand on her table, and her cards scattered.

Bromwyn did not flinch, nor did she tear her gaze away from her mother's brooding eyes. They stared at each other, the air between them thick with unspoken words and emotions too complex to properly name.

It was Bromwyn who broke the silence first. "You must help us," she said plainly. "You simply must, no matter how you feel about it."

"I must do nothing of the sort," her mother said, expertly

gathering her cards. "This is *your* test, Daughter. Not mine."

Bromwyn stiffened.

"So you thought I had no idea, is that it? You thought you could just leave that part out of the problem, did you?" Jessamin laughed, and her eyes shone darkly. "Your grandmother spoke of it to me, before she set off to Mooreston this morning. Your test is upon you. You must fend for yourself, Daughter."

"That is just stupid," Bromwyn growled. "It was not even I who stole the Key!"

"No matter. Your test has come."

"Why? It makes no sense!"

Jessamin watched her for a moment, seemed to weigh something in her mind before she began to shuffle her cards.

"It does," she replied softly. "Eighteen years ago, I was the Guardian during Midsummer. I was tested. And I failed."

"You ... " Bromwyn closed her mouth, uncertain of what to say.

"Failed. Only your grandmother's quick thinking kept the fey from overrunning the village. And I ... " Jessamin glanced down at her hands, which were trembling. She set down her cards in a neat pile, then folded her hands across her lap. "And I lost my magic."

"Mother," Bromwyn said softly, her voice more tender than it had been in a long, long time. "Please tell me—what happened?"

Jessamin lifted her chin. "I failed, and your grandmother tricked the fey and so kept them in line. That is all you need to know."

Neither mother nor daughter said anything for a long moment.

As the silence grew, Bromwyn felt sorry for Jessamin, for the girl her mother had once been and the woman she had never become. Jessamin had lost her magic, and too few years later, she had lost her husband.

The very least Bromwyn could do was make sure she did not lose her dignity as well. So Bromwyn bowed her head and murmured her apology for causing such distress.

*Hasty words,* she thought as she turned away. *Again, I spoke hasty words.*

Lately, it seemed all she did was shout or want to shout at her mother. Perhaps her curse would come again. Perhaps it already had, and that was why her test was upon her now, at the worst possible time she could imagine.

*It is so unfair,* she thought bitterly. But as she was realizing more and more, even when things were unfair, life continued on. Nature had other concerns than the complaints of one witch.

She was halfway out the door before her mother cleared her throat and spoke.

"Your grandmother mentioned that you should teach your friend what you can about the fey. Take my books and help him study. I am certain that with you by his side, your friend will do quite well."

Bromwyn turned to face her mother, dipping her head in acknowledgement of Jessamin's offer. "Thank you," she said sincerely. The books wouldn't solve their problems, but they would at least be helpful—a handful of them would provide Rusty with the primer he needed to handle himself around the fey.

"And Daughter? You will do better at your test than I."

Her voice a strangled whisper, Bromwyn said, "How can you know?"

Jessamin smiled, and her entire face softened as her eyes gleamed with unshed tears. "Because you are my daughter, and I know what you are capable of. My girl, you can do marvelous things. Believe in yourself, for I believe in you."

Then Bromwyn forgot about being sixteen and almost married, and she ran to her mother's side and bent down to hug her tightly, as if that simple act of love could banish all her fears. When Jessamin hugged her just as tightly, everything was right with the world.

Then the moment passed, and the two broke away.

"Go, take what you need," her mother said. "And take my blessing. And know that I love you." Then she arched an eyebrow. "And know that it would not kill you to wash your feet before tonight."

Bromwyn blushed and grinned in equal parts as she strode over to the bookshelf. She rummaged for books about the fey—legend and lore, true accounts and mysteries, poems and songs. As she gathered dusty tomes, she decided right then and there that Rusty, with her help, would be the perfect Guardian. And once Midsummer was done, and the fey were back in their land, and the World Door was once again closed and locked—and Bromwyn passed her test—they would have an entire year to convince Niove to take back the Key.

She nodded to herself. Really, it was quite simple. All she had to do was teach Rusty everything she knew about the fair folk, in roughly eight hours.

And no matter what, she would keep her temper.

Really she would.

# PART 3:

# MIDSUMMER

# MAKING READY

When the sun was an hour's drop away from nightfall, Bromwyn and Rusty met on the outskirts of Master Tiller's spelt fields. Some farming tools lay forgotten on the ground—hoes and sickles and spades, probably dropped in people's haste to get to the center of Loren to take part in the village's Midsummer Festival. If Master Tiller was like most adults, tomorrow he would have strong words with his workers, assuming that he himself wouldn't drink so much ale today that he slept clear through tomorrow evening. Midsummer brews tended to be potent, or so Bromwyn had always heard.

The smell of wheat tickling her nostrils, she hefted her large pack and slung it over her shoulder. Then she grimaced. Fire and Air, the sack was heavy! And that was only with five books stuffed inside. Why did the truly important tomes have to be thick enough to crush bugs?

*Well, no matter,* she told herself. Far more important than her sore back was the chance to review everything one final time before the World Door opened. Still, her back and shoulder ached miserably. She sighed, resigned. She had tried to spell the books to seemingly make them small enough to fit inside a closed fist, but her back had known the difference. No illusion would be strong enough to counter the weight of words. If only she were able to transport the books by using her magic ...

But no, only those of fey blood could fold the air itself and push an object from one place to another by magic alone. The thought made Bromwyn mope.

Her voice curt, she asked Rusty, "You have the blanket?"

"Yes."

"And the bread?"

"Yes."

"And the cheese? And the berries? And the nuts? And the—"

"*Yes,*" Rusty said. "And everything you asked for, I've got. My mam even threw in some of those sugar cookies you love so much." He lowered his voice to mock-whisper: "I think she likes you!"

More likely, Mistress Baker was terrified of her, based on how the woman paled whenever Bromwyn visited the bakery. Before Bromwyn had been apprenticed to her grandmother, Rusty's mother used to give her a packet of sugar cookies for no reason other than to make her smile. "You have a lovely smile, you do," she'd say, handing Bromwyn the treats. But once the cartomancer's daughter had become Lady Witch, the sugar cookies disappeared, as if by magic.

But Bromwyn didn't want to think about how Mistress Baker feared her. "You did not get in trouble for stealing away during the Midsummer rush?"

"Well, yes," he admitted. "Da's threatened to do me in with his rolling pin after the big cleanup tomorrow, but I'm more than half certain he isn't serious. Mam, though—she cried. Said I've broken her heart." He sighed sadly, and then he perked up. "But once I told her of the things I needed, she was happy to help."

Bromwyn frowned at him. "She did not ask any questions?"

Rusty's teeth gleamed as he grinned. "Of course she did. She's a woman, isn't she? Questions are as natural to a woman as curiosity is to a cat."

"Is that so?" she said dryly.

"Indeed. And it's not like I could say to her, 'Mam, I have to impress a bunch of fairy lords and ladies, so can you please fill my basket with any leftovers from this afternoon's trays.' What with fairies not being real, of course."

"Of course."

"So I did the only thing I could to get out of cleanup after the big Midsummer Festival and still get us what we needed." He smiled, and Bromwyn saw a dimple in his right cheek.

Her face warmed as she stared at the tiny flaw. How had she never noticed it before? By Nature's grace, he looked adorable when he smiled so ...

And then he said, "I told her I was planning on wooing you

away from Brend, so I needed to make a nice impression."

Bromwyn choked.

"Hah! Gotcha!" Rusty doubled over from laughter. "You should see your face! Lady Witch, red as a beet!"

That horrid, *horrid* boy. "You," she gasped. "You—!"

He cupped a hand to his ear. "What's that? Can't hear you over all the coughing and spluttering."

Oh, so he couldn't hear her, eh?

Bromwyn cast from the Way of Sound (a close cousin of the Way of Sight, which made it simple for her) and deftly wove a spell around Rusty. She did it so gently that he didn't react to the soft nudge of her magic.

Once the spell was firmly in place, she murmured, "Perhaps I should speak up."

Rusty shrieked like a child upon seeing a snake. Clamping his hands over his ears, he shouted, "Too loud! Too loud!"

"What?" she said innocently. "This, you mean?"

"YES!" He doubled over again, but this time there was no laughter, no guffaws at Bromwyn's expense. He squealed, "Damn me, MAKE IT STOP!"

"As my boy requests." With a swipe of her hand, she unraveled the casting, drawing the energy from the spell into the fertile ground beneath her bare feet. Smiling sweetly, she said, "Got you back."

Rusty tentatively lowered his hands, then he glared at her so fiercely that she should have bled from his cutting gaze. "Masterful control of your temper, Lady Witch."

"That? That was not temper," she said demurely. "That was fun."

"Speak for yourself."

"I am. And besides, you started it."

"It's not my fault you've got no sense of humor," he muttered, sticking one finger in his ear and wiggling it, as if he could shake out the last bits of echo.

"I have a fine sense of humor. See my smile?"

"You're evil, Winnie. Absolutely evil."

Her smile slipped as she said, "I am sure that some in the village would agree." Including her future husband. "Come. We do not have that much time to set up and review."

They walked in silence. At first, Bromwyn was too lost in her swirl of dark thoughts to strike up conversation, but then as the field gave way to the holly trees, silver birches, and rowans that marked the beginning of the woods, she became too enamored of the sights and sensations to even think of small talk. There were the smells, first and foremost—grass and leaf rot and the wild scent of hidden animals, that palpable tang of fur and fear that surrounded all prey, be they hares or squirrels or foxes. Next, the sounds—the churring of nighthawks and whippoorwills, the knocking of woodpeckers, the merry tunes of the skylarks. Beneath her bare feet, the leaf carpet was soft and damp, and more than a little cold, with rough sections of root tendrils threading across the path. Almost as an afterthought, the sights of the woods danced around her: the muted colors of orchid and heather, the bright bluebell and foxglove, all of the flowers winking in the patchy sunlight, ferns and bracken standing waist-high, and the trees, of course—towering above the birches and holly, mighty oaks stood proudly, indifferent to the deadwood of fallen limbs or to the passage of two people walking past them on the well-trod path, a dirt road kept clear of debris by rangers and witches alike.

This was the heart of the Allenswood, home to one of the World Doors, and it was here that Bromwyn, called Darkeyes, felt most at home.

"Creepy," Rusty muttered, as if he were afraid to disrespect the trees.

Bromwyn slid him a look. "If you wish to be a thief, Sir Baker, you should make your peace with the forest." Ignoring his glower, she smiled as she said, "From all the stories, this is where bandits and other lawless fellows make their headquarters."

"I'm more of a rooftop thief."

"And what will you do in towns and villages with thatched roofs?"

"Pass through until I settle in a city with sensible buildings of stone and wood."

"A thief, uneasy in the woods," she said, shaking her head.

"A witch," he sighed, "uneasy with shoes."

"If you worked with Nature, you would not think it odd."

"And if you looked at the state of your feet, you would understand why non-witchy types prefer boots. How far are we going, anyway?"

"A little farther. The clearing is up ahead."

Soon they came to a break in the woods. The glade stretched in an irregular grassy circle, large enough to hold the entirety of Loren's Village Circle and then some. Shrubs and moss dotted the clearing, along with the occasional sapling. The open ground drank the fading sunlight greedily, the greenery shining like emeralds and the grass beneath Bromwyn's feet pleasantly warm after the chill of the forest proper. At the center of the glade stood the Hill with its circle of flat stones.

"We are here," Bromwyn said, gratefully dropping her pack to the ground. "Based on the sun, I would say we have twenty minutes to make ready."

"Plenty of time." Rusty was already unearthing the contents of his sack: a large checkered blanket, bundles of pastries and breads, assorted cheeses, a mixture of nuts and berries, a bottle of apple wine, clay plates for serving, and four copper goblets. He and Bromwyn set out the platters in a pleasing manner (at least, pleasing to Bromwyn's critical eye), and then she murmured a small spell from the Way of Sight that changed the appearance of the plain clay and copper to a delicate silver that she considered more appropriate for fey royalty. The fey would see through the illusion, of course, but she thought they might appreciate the effort. At least, they would be amused by it. That done, she slapped Rusty's hand away from the cheese.

They had perhaps ten minutes to go.

Bromwyn rustled through her pack. "We should review the lore one more time. First, your name will be presented as a matter of course, but neither the King nor Queen will give theirs; they would share something that important only with those they consider their equals. Keep in mind that the fey are not divided by their temperament or by the seasons, as the stories say, and that they all bow to the King and Queen, whose power is without peer. Here, this scholar discusses the various revelries and processions." She flipped through one of the books. "We should reread what he says about Midsummer specifically ... "

"I don't know," Rusty said. "I think that reviewing everything again right now would just make me more nervous than I already am."

" ... actually, no, this is foolish. Wearing one's shirt inside-out will do nothing to offer protection, and if we were to carry any iron tools or wards, they would be gravely offended, and what good would that do?" She tossed aside the book and pulled out another.

"Winnie."

"Here, this one is better." She skimmed, and she spoke as her fingers skipped over the pages. "We do not have enough time to make any charms to help protect us from the fey—the least of those sorts of talismans would take a month to create—but we still should know enough to be polite, and that really is what it comes down to, being polite and not letting them trick us into any agreements—"

"Winnie."

"—because fey bargains are tricky things, and they rarely work out to anyone's advantage other than the fey's." She looked up from the book to met Rusty's gaze. "And even if they seem friendly, they are quick to take offense for the smallest of slights, and their temper is something to be feared. They have been known to go to war for the most trivial of reasons."

"*Winnie,*" he said yet again, but she was not to be stopped; no less than Rusty's life was at stake, not to mention the entire village's existence. And so, Bromwyn continued reviewing the pertinent points.

"Accept nothing from them," she insisted, "no food or drink or treasure, for their gold is charmed and their sustenance will trap you in their land, but neither can you bluntly refuse anything. You must always offer something in return so that no slight is taken. Never offer or accept a fey kiss, lest you be marked for their land, and nothing in this world would keep you healthy and happy until you walked with them through the World Door, and then you would be lost. Never—"

"Never allow a witch to review procedure before a ritual," Rusty said loudly, "lest you be bored to death before the festivities begin."

Bromwyn's mouth hung open for a long moment before she snapped it shut. She distinctly felt the blood pounding in her head as she forced herself to count silently to ten before she responded. The last thing she needed was to have her curse come crashing down upon her; with her luck, it would entail the fey challenging them for the right to walk the world every night for a year.

"Merciful silence." Rusty smiled. "See, this is how it should be."

"Do not tell me how things should be," she said through clenched teeth. "You are this close to having me do something I am certain to regret."

He chuckled softly. "Ah, Winnie. Such sweet things you say.

Brend will be swept off his huge feet."

"This close, I tell you."

"Will you threaten him on your wedding night? Will you scare him so much, he won't come out of the privy?"

"I should turn you into a toad."

"Again with the toad threat. Doesn't it get old? What about turning me into a something else, like a salamander?"

"A toad," she said. "A fat, warty toad. See if your beloved Jalsa will ever kiss those lips when they are covered in warts."

Rusty cocked his head as he seemed to think about it. "If she thought I'd turn into a prince, she probably would."

The two of them stared at each other, and then they both burst out laughing. Bromwyn laughed until her cheeks hurt, and then she laughed even more. The image of the buxom serving girl bent over to kiss a toad was the perfect thing to soothe Bromwyn's frayed nerves. So what that the fey would soon arrive, and that they might bring about the destruction of Loren? So what that Bromwyn's test was upon her, and she still didn't know how she was supposed to pass? So what that she and Rusty were in very real danger of losing their lives—or worse—to the fey? Jalsa kissed the toad-prince, and Bromwyn laughed until her sides ached.

Eventually, laughter gave way to hiccoughing giggles, and then the two friends sat down on the blanket. Smoothing her skirt, Bromwyn wondered if Brend would ever make her laugh the way that Rusty did.

It didn't matter, though. She was promised to the smith's apprentice, and she would marry him.

Bromwyn's eyes stung. She, like her mother, would lead a loveless life. And Rusty, like his father, would simply be a baker, no matter where his heart longed to go. Children didn't have the option of choosing their life's work—at least, not in Loren. Perhaps in other villages, in other lands, they did. But here, their destinies were laid out for them in the forms of their fathers and mothers.

"Copper for your thoughts, Winnie."

She forced herself to smile. "I was thinking that I wish we could change things."

"Ah, don't you fret," Rusty said, patting her hand. "We'll be fine. This is but the first of our many adventures."

This time, the smile wasn't forced at all. "Really?"

"Sure. Why, soon enough the whole world will spin the tales of Lord Thief and Lady Witch." Grinning, he launched into the story of their next heroic saga: After conquering the fairies, they would run away and steal a ship, then make their way to the castle of the merfolk and go on to become fabled pirates.

Bromwyn listened, and laughed, and applauded when his tale was done. As much as she wished they could just run away, Bromwyn knew she was as bound to Loren as Rusty was. No matter how much they wanted it, they could not change their place in the scheme of things. So though she smiled, her heart was as heavy as the immobile stones that marked the World Door—stones that had begun to shimmer in the fading light.

The fey were coming.

# THE WORLD DOOR OPENS

Bromwyn let out a shaky breath. On the Hill, the large, flat stones of the fey ring seemed to wink as they reflected the golds and reds of the setting sun.

"We have a few minutes more," she said. "Do you know what to do?"

Rusty grinned, but clearly it was to hide a scream. He was sweating through his collar, and there was a nervous sheen to his eyes. "Besides pray that we won't get killed too badly, you mean?"

She smiled in an attempt to calm his nerves. It didn't help that she was sitting on her hands to keep from wringing them. "Besides that."

"The three double-yous, right? Words of welcome, words of warning, words of wisdom."

"Right," she said, nodding. "And then?"

"The fourth double-you. The wine."

"Yes. And?"

"Er." His brow furrowed, and he removed his hat to rake his fingers through his unruly red hair. "'And?' There's an 'and?'"

Of course he'd miss the most important bit. Sometimes, Rusty could be such a *boy*. "You need to present them with the Key."

He rolled his eyes, and then he jammed his hat back onto his head. "Well, of course. That's part of the welcome, isn't it?"

"It is separate from the welcome," she said patiently. Or as patiently as she could, when what she wanted to do was smack the side of his head. "You need to show them the proof of office."

"What proof of office?"

"The *Key*, Rusty! You are the Key Bearer, so you need to show them the Key!"

Rusty blinked. "That's a stupid way of calling it. 'Proof of office.' It's proof of no such thing."

"It is proof that your so-called luck has finally turned southerly," Bromwyn said, and when Rusty rolled his eyes at her again, she added, "It is proof that perhaps you should consider another profession for when you finally grow up!"

She didn't realize that she was shouting until she heard her own voice echoing through the clearing.

"Much obliged, Mistress Smith," Rusty said dryly. "Pray tell, did you give out such advice when you were merely Lady Witch, she of the filthy feet and overbearing manner?"

She glared at him, and never mind how she peripherally saw that the flat stones of the Hill now seemed to glow. "If I did not care about you so much, I would cast a spell to make you bald!"

"So? My hat would still cover my head."

"And instead of 'Rusty,' you would be 'Baldy.' Or ... something even worse!"

"So you care about me, eh?"

Bromwyn stared at him, her mouth agape, before she regained her composure. "Of course I do," she said. "You are my friend." A true friend. And, truth be told, her only friend.

"Aw." He grinned at her, showing far too many teeth. "I think you like me!"

"And I think you are an idiot." She sniffed. "You need my help, so I am helping."

"Lady Witch is too kind."

"As you say." She took a deep breath. "Come. It is time."

His face paled, but he stretched his grin tighter upon his face. "All right. Let's show these fairies there's a new Key Bearer at the Door."

He held out his hand to her, and she took it; his hand was damp, but his grip was strong. Her heart thumped hard enough that her chest ached—but as scared as she was for Rusty and for herself, she was also the teensiest bit excited. They would do this. Rusty would be the perfect Guardian, and she would pass her test. The fey would leave them no worse for wear, and Loren would be none the wiser. It was better than knowing the juiciest secret about the most proper village elders.

Fire and Air, Rusty's wicked ways were rubbing off on her.

Grinning back at him, she said, "As you say, Lord Guardian."

Together they stood and faced the Hill. The stones sparkled now, and stars twinkled over them in a line, shaping the impression of a door. Or, in this case, a Door: a path between realities.

Pulling her hand from Rusty's and keeping her gaze on the brightening portal, she said, "Do you have the Key?"

"Yes."

"And you know what to say?"

There was a pained sigh, and he said, "Yes."

"And you know what to do?"

"*Yes.* Damn me, Winnie, you're not starting this again, are you?"

"Sorry."

As the Door became more solid, she prayed to Nature that she would do her mother and grandmother proud. Or, she amended, at least not get killed. To face her grandmother after Niove resurrected her would literally be a fate worse than death. And Bromwyn would never hear the end of it.

Rusty whispered, "Winnie?"

"Yes?"

"Thanks for being here." And then he kissed her cheek.

She would have responded—even with her words stuck in her throat, she certainly would have replied—but then the line of stars blazed. Bromwyn sensed, more than saw, Rusty flinch and look away. She, herself, kept her gaze fixed on the Door, grinning hugely, and all she could think for that one moment was: *He kissed me he kissed me he kissed me!*

There was only that thought, and the sound of leaves rustling in the trees around them, and the stars dancing on the stones. And for that one shining moment, Bromwyn Elmindrea Lucinda Moon, called Darkeyes, was the happiest girl in the world.

And then the World Door opened.

The thunderous *BOOM* whipped Bromwyn's hair and dress, echoing through her body until her teeth shook and her skull thrummed, but she was a witch upon the brink of her test, so she stood tall and didn't look away as the power that defined all the realms of all the worlds roared around her. The line of white light was now a wide gap, like a tear—and the white wasn't truly white, but rather all of the colors of the world and some from beyond the world, shimmering and sparkling like captured magic. It was beautiful and wild and altogether fascinating. The Door beckoned, and part of Bromwyn longed to answer.

If it tugged at *her*, what was it doing to Rusty?

She darted a glance at him. Rusty was on one knee, his hands clamped on his ears, his teeth clenched as if to keep from screaming. What she heard as a *BOOM* must have been deafening to him—the sound of reality forming was a thing that made even gods uncomfortable, so it was said, and here was Rusty, a sixteen-year-old human boy, standing in the path of the force that shaped the universe. Bromwyn dearly hoped it wouldn't drive him mad.

*I will keep you safe*, she promised him, trying to push the thought into his head, as if she were able to walk the fabled Way of the Mind. If he heard her, she could not tell. *The sound passes*, she tried to think at him.

She was correct: Already the earth-shaking crash was abating, replaced with the sound of raucous laughter. It was loud and infectious, and as the mirth washed over her, Bromwyn had to fight to keep a smile from tugging the corners of her mouth. Peripherally, she saw Rusty lift his head up and lower his hands from his ears, a tentative grin on his face. She nodded, once, to herself; for the moment, her friend was all right. The day Rusty ignored laughter was the day he was doomed.

A swarm of bees surged through the painfully bright light of the stars on the stones. Rusty yelped and ducked his head, but Bromwyn kept her chin high and her gaze focused on the open Door. Buzzing with laughter, the bees spun drunkenly around her before moving past. Those that halted in front of her shimmered and sparkled—and grew. No longer insect-sized, Bromwyn saw that they were human-shaped, with gossamer wings fluttering wildly. Some remained tiny, barely the size of her small finger. Others swelled to adult-human size. Still others grew even larger. All were enticingly beautiful, almost too lovely to look upon. All had a mop of blond hair and piercingly blue eyes, and all were adorned with flowers. They danced in the air, laughing, pointing at her and Rusty, inviting them to come play.

She wondered if one of them was Nala from so long ago.

Bromwyn gritted her teeth and dug her heels into the ground. Tonight she was the Wise One of Loren, and she would not be tempted, not by pixies or any other fey creature.

As if a signal had been given, the fey sighed as one, and the sound was like the wind rustling through the trees. Then they parted, leaving a clear path from Bromwyn and Rusty to the Door.

Next to her, Rusty scrambled to his feet. She felt, more than saw, as he threw a glance at her, so she turned her head slightly, just enough to see him looking right at her, his mouth fixed in a huge grin. He winked at her, and then he looked straight at the Door.

Fire and Air, the boy could be so infuriating!

No time to think on that, though, for two figures were soaring through the Door. These two had no wings, yet they stepped on the air itself, and Bromwyn felt an old pang of jealousy surge through her. As it was when she had been eleven, so these two were now dressed: The woman was clothed in flowers and silk, and her long green hair shone with diamonds; holding her hand, the blond man wore blue silks and a cape of flowers, with a crown of silver glinting on his brow.

The Queen and King of the fey hovered before Bromwyn, amused smiles on their faces and something close to hunger in their eyes.

*I am the granddaughter of Niove Whitehair,* Bromwyn reminded herself. *I am Bromwyn, called Darkeyes, and tonight I am the Wise One of Loren.*

*I am unafraid.*

With that thought, she stood a little taller and she smiled, even though she wanted to run away as fast as she could.

# THE LORD GUARDIAN

"My lord husband," said the Queen, her sapphire eyes sparkling wickedly as she stared at Bromwyn, "it was my understanding that there would be a Guardian at the Door."

"Mine as well, my lady wife," said the King, whose own gaze was more like the icy skies of winter. "But instead of the ancient Whitehair, I see two children."

"A boy child," the Queen purred, "who sweats from nerves and grins so deliciously."

"And young Darkeyes," the King said. "What an unexpected surprise. Still a child, but on the cusp of adulthood."

"For her kind," said the Queen, with a sly look at her husband.

"Both of them, almost of age," he replied, his smile pulling into something frightening.

Even though Bromwyn's stomach rolled and her heart felt

squeezed tight and her throat wanted to close up, she curtsied deeply and announced in a clear voice: "My lady and lord of the fey, welcome to the Allenswood."

"She speaks," said the Queen, bemused. "Perhaps she does other tricks as well. Perhaps she will come when called, or roll over for a good word."

"Or beg." The King grinned at Bromwyn, and what she saw in that grin and in his wintery blue eyes made her feel slightly sick. Or maybe that was because they were comparing her to a dog.

Keeping her smile locked on her face, Bromwyn said, "It is my pleasure to present to you the Key Bearer and Guardian of the Allenswood World Door, he who is also your host. Majesties, here before you is Derek Jonasson."

And she thought, *By Nature's grace, please do not mess this up.* Whether that thought was to herself or to Rusty, she could not have said.

Rusty stepped forward, removing his hat with one practiced gesture and bowing smoothly. "At your service," he said to his belly.

The glade quieted, from the wind in the leaves to the fey horde in attendance, as the King and Queen considered Rusty. The two rulers didn't move, save for the expressions on their faces. The Queen's mouth slid from a surprised *O* to a delighted smile, and she actually clapped her hands together like a child receiving a wonderful gift. The King's face seemed to move in reverse—his grin tightened, then slipped away altogether, and his eyes narrowed as he looked first at Rusty, then at Bromwyn. Those eyes seemed to frost with ice, leeching out the blue and leaving a scum of dirty white.

"You mean to say that the Whitehair is not coming at all?" The King's voice dripped with scorn. "And in her stead, she sends us this whelp and this unworldly slip of a girl?"

Though she sensed the King's building anger—he must have been insulted by Niove's absence—it paled before Bromwyn's own budding rage. Unworldly, indeed!

"My grandmother selected the new Guardian with great care," she said politely, keeping her smile in place. "And she sends her regards."

He snorted his derision. "I am less than impressed."

Fury burned through Bromwyn, but she kept her face calm even as white-hot heat scalded her from within. *Keep your temper,* she told herself. *Whatever else you do, keep your temper.*

The Queen was moving now, gliding in the air to hover around Rusty, circling him as if he were a horse to be bought. Rusty held his bow, but Bromwyn saw the slight tremble along his arms.

"The boy is a fine one," the Queen murmured. "He will look delightful in my Court."

"The boy is too thin," commented the King. "He will break in less than a fortnight."

The Queen arched a brow at him. "Is that a wager?"

"Perhaps. What will you offer?"

"Majesties," Bromwyn said tightly, "I understand your surprise. But it seems to this unworldly girl that your surprise now borders on rudeness. There is a decorum to be followed, should you wish to remain on our land for this Midsummer Festival."

The sudden hush through the clearing was thick and suffocating, and if Bromwyn hadn't been so furious from the King's scorn and the Queen's bemusement, she would have been terrified. Angering the fey was far from smart. But she couldn't just stand there and let them insult her and Rusty. If she didn't show them her spine now, they would walk all over her—and that would be only the beginning. Bromwyn didn't want to think about what they would do after that. She held her chin high and waited for their response.

After what felt like a million years, the King said, "You are correct, witchling." His voice boomed through the glade like summer thunder rumbling in the mountains. "My lady wife and I have overstepped, and for that we offer our apologies."

Next to Rusty, the Queen said nothing, but she bowed her head ever so slightly.

Bromwyn opened her mouth, but it was Rusty who spoke first.

"Your apologies are most graciously acknowledged," he said, standing tall once again. "But majesties, they are unnecessary. Of course your graces were surprised by our presence here. You are used to the dread power of our Wise One, Niove Whitehair. And I am but a young man, and the Lady Witch is not her grandmother. For causing such surprise, I most humbly offer our own apologies, which I sincerely hope you will accept in the manner in which they are offered: freely, with no ill intention."

Bromwyn blinked at him, her mouth hanging open wide enough to swallow some of the tinier fey creatures buzzing near her. By Nature's grace, what in all the realms was possessing her friend? He spoke the perfect words, far smoother than her own meager attempt at diplomacy. He ...

... was quoting from one of the books they had studied earlier that day.

Bromwyn's mouth snapped shut as she remembered the chapter from the massive tome on court etiquette that they had reviewed. Come to think of it, Rusty had taken longer with that book than he had with the others. And now Bromwyn knew why: He had been memorizing key phrases.

Well, assuming they both survived this encounter with the fey, perhaps she could convince him to pursue acting instead of thievery.

"Well spoken, young master," the Queen said with a full-lipped smile. "How could we do other than as you request? My lord husband and I graciously accept your thoughtful apology, for you and the witch girl both."

Bromwyn's eyes narrowed. She didn't care for how the Queen was smiling at Rusty. No, not at all.

"You are most kind, lady Queen," said Rusty. "May I present to you my proof of office?" He pulled out the Key from his pocket and displayed it on his palm as if it were the greatest of treasures.

"It seems you are indeed the Key Bearer," the King said flatly.

"My lord Guardian," said the Queen, her voice breathy, and she even curtsied before Rusty. "For a young man to carry such a burden, there must be far more to you than meets the eye." She looked up from her curtsey and smiled once again, her lips shining wetly in the starlight of the World Door. "I look forward to discovering your hidden talents, my lord Guardian."

Bromwyn's fists shook. The Queen was ... flirting! With Rusty! Who was grinning like a fool! And blushing!

If his wife's mannerisms bothered him at all, the King did not show it. "The Key to the World Door is many things," said the King, "and one of them is iron. And so we must ask, Key Bearer, that you replace the Key in your pocket and keep it there until the time should come for it to be used."

"Speaking of such a time," said Bromwyn, glaring at Rusty, "we must state the rules of your visit this fine evening."

"*We* must do no such thing, witchling," the King said jovially. His eyes now sparkled as brightly as his lady wife's; the anger that had danced there was gone. "Only the Key Bearer may act as the Guardian of your land. You are merely an amusement, nothing more."

The words slapped Bromwyn. Eyes stinging with unshed tears, she gritted her teeth and said nothing as she silently raged.

"Thank you, my lord King, for reminding me of my responsibilities," Rusty said smoothly. "Your lady Queen was so charming that I nearly forgot myself."

"My lord Guardian is quite the flatterer," the Queen said, lips curled in a smile that hinted at many things.

Bromwyn wanted to rip that smile off of the Queen's face. *Stop looking at him that way!*

The Queen's lips pulled wider, almost as if she could hear Bromwyn's furious thoughts.

"Lady Witch," Rusty said, "would you be so kind as to pour the wine?"

Bromwyn tore her gaze away from the Queen and met Rusty's intense stare. His eyes implored her to please, please, *please* keep her temper.

"As the lord Guardian requests," she said, her tone clipped.

Rusty dipped his head in acknowledgement. "Thank you." He didn't add "Winnie," but Bromwyn could see the nickname on his lips.

Somehow, just sensing the shape of his pet name for her made her less angry, and it was with a tight smile that she turned her back on the fey royalty to open the cask of wine.

As she prepared the cups, Rusty made small talk with the Queen and King, and even with some of the watching fey folk. Bromwyn didn't know how he could be so at ease. She'd nearly lost her temper more than once, and the fey had been there for not even five minutes. And yet, there was Rusty, holding his own, charming the Queen, even joking with the King. Thank Nature for small favors.

She filled the four goblets with the apple wine. The Guardian had to toast the fey King and Queen, but before the first taste of wine was sipped, the rules of decorum had to be clearly stated as well as agreed to by the fey. Once the wine was sipped, those rules—and only those rules—would be enforced. If the Guardian didn't impress the King and Queen during their visit, there was the very real threat of them challenging the Guardian's authority.

And that, as Rusty would have said, would be very bad.

Biting her lip, Bromwyn corked the bottle. No, she would not worry. Rusty knew what to do.

Carefully, she brought over all four goblets. Rusty took two from her, and then the two of them presented the cups to the fey sovereigns. The King and Queen exchanged a bemused look, and then they each selected a cup—the King from Bromwyn, the Queen from Rusty.

"I should like to wish you blessings and prosperity," Rusty said, "but everyone knows that the fey are already blessed and prosperous. And so I wish friendship between our peoples on this Midsummer night. And in the name of that friendship, let no human child be stolen this night by the fey or otherwise marked by the fey, and let no human adult be taken for any reason by the fey."

*Perfect.* Bromwyn smiled to herself. He said it just as they had practiced. The first rule, and by far the most important, had been stated. Now the fey had to accept the conditions Rusty had set forth.

"Well spoken," the Queen murmured. "We do solemnly agree to your most reasonable request, my lord Guardian."

One rule down, and only about a thousand more to go. But Bromwyn wasn't daunted. They could do this.

Around them, the fey cheered. From somewhere, drums began to beat a wild rhythm, one that captured the feeling of a hunter chasing prey through the lush woods. Bromwyn felt the music's effects on her body—the way her heart seemed to mimic the drumbeat, how her limbs wanted to move and caper and dance. She forced her feet to remain still.

"Our children celebrate," the King said, his voice a rich bass that was a musical accompaniment to the music. "We should do no less. Come, witchling." He plucked Bromwyn's cup from her hand and thrust it and his own goblet to the Queen, who used her magic to float the additional cups gently in the air.

"My lord?" Bromwyn stammered. "What are you doing?"

"It has been far too long." The King took Bromwyn by the elbow. "Let us fly once again and dance beneath the stars."

Before she could say anything else, the King's magic washed over her—and suddenly, Bromwyn was flying as the King held her aloft. Her stomach dropped to her toes and her heart thumped loudly in her chest. Bromwyn didn't know whether the sound that escaped her lips was a groan or a giggle.

They danced.

"Five years ago," the King murmured, "I offered you your heart's desire. And you refused me."

Bromwyn swallowed thickly before she replied. "It was a most generous offer, my lord. But the price was too high."

"You would have had a place in my Court as my daughter. Was it so much to ask that you love me with all of your heart, young Darkeyes?"

"Yes, my lord."

"And now? At the cusp of adulthood, have you found another to whom you would give your heart?"

"I am betrothed, my lord."

A smile played on the King's lips, hinting at amusement. "You have learned how to reply to a question without actually answering it. Well done. Now answer me truly, witchling: Is there another to whom you have given your heart?"

For some reason, she briefly thought of Rusty, who even now was alone with the Queen and her charms, the Queen and her lush smiles.

She pushed thoughts of him aside; she didn't have the luxury of being concerned for her friend, not when the King had charged her to speak the truth. She admitted, "I have been promised to someone, my lord. My heart is no longer mine to give."

"You wear your sorrow like a scarf, witchling. It screams to be noticed, even as it strangles you. You are unhappy here, in this land that my kith and kin visit once each year."

She found she could no longer meet his gaze.

"In my land," he said gently, "you would have your pick of fey suitors. Any who would ask for your heart would be yours, with only a word of consent from you. In my land, you would never have to pledge your heart to another if you did not wish it."

"Except to you, my lord."

"Except to me," he agreed, "and to my lady Queen. But I promise you this, Bromwyn Darkeyes: In my land, you would want nothing less. In my land, surrounded by all the joys and desires that magic provides, you would be content, and more than content. You would be happy."

She thought of how peaceful she felt when she walked barefoot through the Allenswood, and she wondered, as she danced through the air with the fey King, what it would be like to walk in a place where magic and Nature had wed.

She bit her lip, and then in a small voice, she asked, "Are ... are you offering me a place in your land, my lord?"

He leaned down, as if to kiss her cheek, but instead he whispered in her ear:

"No. You refused me, and I told you that I would never offer such a prize to you again. I am simply letting you know just how wrong your choice was. You will never be happy here, witchling, in your world where magic is looked at with suspicion. You will grow old with bitterness in your heart, knowing that you could have been happy forever in my land. You will die, wasted and alone, and all your potential will be gone, with nothing to show for it."

Bromwyn squeezed her eyes shut, but still the tears came.

The King's laughter was cruel and cutting, and as they floated back down to the forest, Bromwyn felt something vital inside of her slowly bleed away.

Once her feet were on the ground, she pulled away from the King and sank to her knees, sobbing. Her body shook as she cried, and soon her sobbing gave way to coughing. She tried to calm herself, but she found she could not take a proper breath.

Around her, the fey horde laughed and danced to the beat of wild drums.

A hand pressed down upon her shoulder.

"Here, Winnie." It was Rusty who spoke, his voice filled with concern. "Drink this."

Something was put into her hand—a cup. Coughing, she drank. She swallowed apple wine.

Her coughing vanished, as if by magic.

Eyes wide, she stared at the ritual cup. *Oh no,* she thought. *No no no no no…*

"My children," the King said, raising his arms high. "The only rule is that which you heard: No human child may be stolen this night or otherwise marked, and no human adult may be taken for any reason."

The fey buzzed with malicious glee.

Bromwyn's goblet slid from her numb fingers. Wine splashed at her feet and stained her dress.

"Clothe yourselves properly," the Queen declared. "After all, we must blend in if we are to make mischief." With a wave of her hand, two images appeared.

Bromwyn gasped as she gazed upon the likenesses of Brend and Jalsa, both of them grinning wickedly, as if they longed to do evil things.

The Queen said, "These are the images in the forefront of the lord Guardian's mind. Wear them."

The fey shimmered and rippled, and then the glade was filled with hundreds of copies of Brend and Jalsa.

Bromwyn shoved her fists into her mouth to keep from crying out.

"I don't understand," Rusty said to her, sounding panicked. "What's happening here? What are they doing?"

"The evening is yours," the King announced. "Enjoy the night! And know that at the blue hour, we will see our Key Bearer answer our challenge. Fly!"

Spewing laughter, the fey burst from the clearing and scattered in the night, leaving Bromwyn and Rusty with the King and Queen.

"I don't understand," Rusty said again, this time sounding angry as well as scared.

"We were most impressed by your honeyed words, my lord Guardian," said the Queen, turning the honorific into a mocking title. "But we do not believe you have any power behind them."

"We thank you most humbly for leaving the fey to their own devises in matters of conduct," the King said with a laugh, taking the Queen's hand in his own. "Barring, of course, stealing children and luring adults."

"Which comes as little surprise. Anyone would know to place those restrictions upon us," said the Queen.

"Indeed," said the King. "The Whitehair was never so trusting, not in all of her long years as Guardian. And yet, here you are, with no further rules. And with barely a trick from us."

"You said she was choking!" Rusty shouted. "You said she needed something to soothe her throat!"

"Indeed I did. And you gave her the wine to drink. And so the terms for the rules have come to a close." The Queen smiled, poisonously sweet. "You understand that we must press our claim to your land."

"No," Bromwyn whispered.

"Yes," said the King, and then he and the Queen began to dance in the air.

"It has been too many years since the fey have freely walked your world when it was not the magic of Midsummer," said the Queen as she and the King leapt on the wind.

"And we long to do so again," said the King as they spun in a circle.

"It is clear that the witch girl hoped we would not challenge you, my lord Guardian." The Queen laughed richly. "But challenge you we shall, and you will meet it with good grace."

"Come," said the King to the Queen as they danced. The scent of honeysuckle in the rain filled the glen as the Queen's hair and King's cape blew in the breeze. "Let us explore as we have not done in more than a human's age." He turned to grin at Bromwyn. "Upon our return, we shall see if once again we may dance upon these skies every night for the next year."

"And introduce our ways to your lovely village," said the Queen, grinning hungrily. "Until the blue hour, my lord Guardian!"

The King chortled, "Until the blue hour, witchling!"

With that, they were gone.

"This," Rusty said, looking up into the sky, "is really bad, isn't it?"

"Yes," Bromwyn said thickly. "It really is. The fey are going to bring Loren to its knees tonight. And just before dawn, the King and Queen will challenge you for the right to keep open the World Door for a whole year." She swallowed. This was her test—she knew it in her darkest heart. It was already a disaster, and she feared that no matter what she did now, she would lose her magic. And that would only be the start. She whispered, "Grandmother is going to kill me. A lot."

"Are you speaking figuratively, or literally?"

She didn't reply.

The sounds of the fey shrieking laughter tore the nighttime sky.

Bromwyn finally shook herself free from her despair, took a deep breath and pulled herself to her feet. "Come on. We have to get moving."

"Why? Are we running away?"

"Running toward. We have to get back to the village before the fey do too much damage."

Rusty looked down at his boots. "I liked my answer better by far."

# FIGHTING FIRE WITH FIRE

The two of them raced through the Allenswood, desperate to get back to the village. Their feet skimmed over tree roots and the leaf carpet of the woods as they dashed so quickly that they nearly flew. Their way was lit by a hasty spell from the Way of Sight on Bromwyn's hand, which now glowed as if she cupped a star in her palm; holding her arm up as if it were a torch, she illuminated their way. On they ran, incited by the fey drums and the urgency of the moment—the Guardian chasing after his charges and the would-be Wise One with twigs and bits of leaf caught in her long hair. Bromwyn was certain they would make it back to the village in time to put an end to the worst of the damage.

Perhaps that would have happened, had some of the fey not remained in the forest, ready to make mischief.

With a splintery roar, the Allenswood came alive to intercept

Bromwyn and Rusty. Tree branches barred their way in a wall of bark and leaves; to their sides, tanglers burst from the ground, thick and green and flowing like snakes; behind them, thorns weaved their way between knee-high bushes, ready to cut tender flesh.

The friends skidded to a halt.

"This way," Rusty shouted, pulling Bromwyn to the left. He drew a long knife from his boot and started hacking a path through the tanglers.

From her belt, Bromwyn pulled out her own knife, normally used for slicing cheese and fruit, and she joined Rusty in cutting through the ropey foliage. The bell-like sound of fey laughter infuriated her, and she stabbed the greenery in violent strokes.

The tanglers sagged and retreated from the savagery of their attack, and the two friends pushed their way through.

On they ran, until an adventurous branch snagged Bromwyn's long skirt and sent her sprawling. Her spell of light unraveled as she crashed to the ground, and in the dark she gasped as the severed magic surged through her.

Around her, safely hidden, the fey giggled.

From the blackness behind her, Rusty shouted: "Winnie!"

"Here," she growled, clenching her teeth against the searing wave of wild magic. With a grunt, she reached inside herself and channeled that force into the leafy ground. A moment later, the pain dissipated.

Shaking from exertion and fear, Bromwyn once again cast from the Way of Sight, and once again, her right hand glowed.

"You all right?" Rusty asked, offering her a hand to help her up.

Before she could answer or even accept his aid, brambles erupted from the ground and sliced the meat of his palm. He cried out, spraying Bromwyn in droplets of blood as he yanked his hand back.

The fey chortled.

She didn't know which enraged her more: seeing her friend injured or hearing the mocking laughter of the fey. It didn't matter; she'd had enough. With a snarl, Bromwyn cast from the Way of Taste, weaving her spell deftly and quickly as the anger coursing through her goaded her to work faster than ever while using a Way other than Sight.

The jeering laughter soon turned to harsh coughing as the fey felt the effects of her magic. It was a taste she knew quite well, for there were many times over the years when her grandmother had washed Bromwyn's mouth out with soap. The price of speaking her mind had been a very clean palate.

Still coughing, more than a dozen pixies burst from the cover of the trees, flying up past the leaf canopy and into the night.

Bromwyn hoped that none of them were Nala.

"Nasty little things," Rusty growled, sucking the blood from his hand.

"The fey can be vicious. But then, so can we." Yanking her skirt free, Bromwyn realized that she used her magic out of anger. Well, she had other worries bigger than her curse—and besides, she was already feeling resentful and bitter and the icy touch of fear, so what else could the curse possibly do to her? She asked, "How is your hand?"

"Stings, but I'll live."

At least, he would for the moment; what would happen once her grandmother returned was anyone's guess.

"Come on," she said, grabbing his other hand. "We have to hurry."

They ran.

Ten minutes later, as they approached Master Tiller's abandoned farm, Bromwyn thought they still had a chance to rein in the fey before things got out of control. Seeing a light in the fields, she carefully unraveled the spell on her hand, assuming that the farmer had hung covered candles to celebrate Midsummer. Then she realized it was not a light within the rows of spelt but the stalks themselves glowing brighter than they ever did during the day, let alone at night.

And then she smelled smoke.

"Fire!" she shouted, pointing to the orange glow amid the fields.

She and Rusty dashed to the farmer's water pump, which stood next to a row of large buckets. Bromwyn worked the machine to fill one of the pails halfway, which Rusty then hefted to the field to douse the flames.

Bromwyn starting filling another bucket.

"This isn't going to work," he shouted as Bromwyn worked furiously. "It didn't do anything to even this tiny lick of fire here!"

"It has to work," she yelled over the sound of the water spurting into her pail. "It is all we can do!"

"You're a witch! Use your magic!"

"I am a witch of the Way of Sight," she shouted. "What am I

supposed to do, trick the fire with an illusion of guttering out?"

He called back, "Sounds good to me!"

Bromwyn growled her frustration and dropped the half-full bucket to the ground. The water sloshed over the edges, but most of it remained inside the pail.

She snarled at the water, as if it were the cause of all her problems. Rusty didn't understand; it wasn't as if she were some storybook witch, able to tame the forces of Nature itself with barely a thought. No, that sort of might was reserved for creatures *of* magic, like the fey. It wasn't meant for some human girl who was simply able to work *with* magic.

She stomped her foot. What she wouldn't give to have real power—to fly through the air, or to have the rains fall from the sky at her command. But she had learned her lessons well, far too well. From everything her grandmother had taught her, along with knowing how to work magic, she had to *believe* that her magic would do what she wanted it to do. And Bromwyn knew that casting from Sight would not put out a fire. For that matter, casting from any of the Ways of Witchcraft would be a waste of time and effort.

Wait, that might not be true. She frowned, thinking. Maybe she could attempt to cast from the Way of Death—literally kill the fire.

But even though she had studied all of the Ways of Witchcraft, she had never tried to cast from that particular path. If she failed, the results could be far worse than Master Tiller losing his livelihood. She could accidentally suck out all the life around her and blight the land. Vexed, she blew out an angry sigh. No, she couldn't take that risk, not without her grandmother there to guide her.

Then what? She had to do *something*.

Rusty ran up to her, barking out a series of coughs. "Some magic would be good, and now, if you please!"

"Fire and Air," she muttered, and then she blinked. She swore by Fire all the time. That meant she believed in its power … didn't it?

Did she believe in its power enough to cast from it, as if Fire were a Way of Witchcraft?

Screwing up her courage—or maybe just her bravado—she turned to face the burning fields. Reaching deep inside of herself, she closed her eyes and touched the core of her power, the place where her magic lived, where it connected her to all of Nature. She held onto that magic, let it fill her almost to the bursting point, and then she cast it out onto the fields. It blanketed the rows of spelt, and she felt as it rode the wind—Air—and then touched the grain—Earth—and then sizzled around the fire.

*Fire.*

Her eyes were closed, but she easily saw and felt the flames around her, trying to burn her, cleanse her, char her and free her to drift like smoke. Instead of shrinking from such power or swatting it away, she welcomed it, taking it deep inside herself—and then she tried to quash it. Sweat beaded on her brow, her neck, her arms. The air she breathed scorched her lungs.

"Winnie?" Rusty's voice sounded strained and scared. "I think you're on fire … "

Bromwyn bit her lip as she pushed the Fire back.

It reared up and sought to roast her alive.

"Water," she wheezed.

A moment later, she was dripping from head to foot; Rusty must have upended the bucket over her. But still the Fire roared, both in the fields and inside of Bromwyn. The feeble amount of water from the pail wouldn't be nearly enough to quench the inferno around her or within her.

Now there was something else on her: hands patting her. That had to be Rusty again, probably trying to smother the fire with his jacket. But she knew it wouldn't work.

She cursed silently and wondered if she was going to die.

And then she cursed again, the words chiming like bells: *Fire and Air!*

Air.

She released the Fire and grabbed for the winds, and they answered. Air buffeted her, whipped her wet hair and dress, overpowering the magical fire until it was nothing more than tingles on her skin. The winds rolled around her, moving faster and faster, and she cast them out and over Master Tiller's fields. The gales roared in delight, and Bromwyn laughed with them as Air blanketed Fire and smothered it.

Once the flames were snuffed out completely, Bromwyn released the Air, and she sighed as it blended into the nighttime sky, its power once again one with Nature.

And then her body felt like her mother had hung her up like a rug and thrashed all the dirt off of her, and her head felt fuzzy, and her thoughts were soupy and slow. She tumbled against Rusty and said, "Ow."

He lowered her down gently, and for a moment she just lay there on the ground, her head in Rusty's lap and his hand brushing her sweaty curls away from her face, and she breathed, and she allowed herself both to hurt and to enjoy the feeling of Rusty holding her so close.

And then she took a deep breath and pushed away both the pain and the pleasure. For tonight, she was the Wise One of Loren. She'd made a mess of things, and she had to clean them up. After that was done, she could collapse for a week in bed. And that was assuming neither the fey nor her grandmother killed her first.

She looked up at Rusty. "Thank you."

"You were amazing," he said, his voice dreamy. "Bromwyn Darkeyes, you were … " He shook his head. "Winnie, I don't have the words. Just … wow."

"A good wow? Or a bad wow?"

"Good wow. Definitely a good wow."

She smiled, wishing she could stay in his arms for even a moment more. But she had a job to do. They both did. She murmured, "You are a silly boy."

"Boy?" His eyes sparkled as he grinned at her. "I'm a man, just as you're a woman."

"What I am is exhausted." Her smile faded, and as she gazed into Rusty's eyes, she said solemnly, "But I am also a witch, and you are the Guardian during Midsummer, and we have to help the villagers handle the fey."

Something dark passed over Rusty's face, but it was fleeting, and then all Bromwyn could see in his eyes was mischief.

"Come on, then," he said. "Stop lying about, you lazy thing. We've got fairies to catch."

# CHILD'S PLAY

Approaching the main avenue of Loren, Bromwyn and Rusty saw just how bad things truly were.

In their iron baskets, the streetlamps were all ablaze, as if the fey had purposely left the suspended lanterns burning so that the people of Loren could fully appreciate the damage. Doors were smashed; wooden fences, ruined. Goods had been scattered to the wind. Apples littered the muddy streets, as if a mighty gale had blown through the village's orchard and scattered the fruit like marbles. Debris and wreckage dotted the road, and Bromwyn stepped carefully around broken earthenware urns and jars. As she picked her way along the street, she recognized the remains of a cheese press and the dented forms of a multitude of strainers and pans. Yellow dust swirled like a golden tempest, and Bromwyn understood that the village's wooden barn that stored its grain had been shattered. Loren stank like scorched earth.

And it looked like utter madness. People ran through the muddy streets, screaming as dozens of copies of Brend and Jalsa soared through the air, taunting the grownups and terrorizing the animals. Livestock bleated and whinnied and brayed, and just as the grownups ran amok, so did the pigs and the oxen and the chickens and the sheep and the cows. Cats loitered, strangely undisturbed, as everyone and everything else fell to chaos. Here the fey buzzed about, some flying, some on foot, all laughing and using their magic to trip or sting the human adults; there the fey dragged people from their homes and peppered them with stones, or with the very Midsummer offerings that had been left for them earlier that day. The villagers whimpered as the fey pelted them with rotten fruit and stale bread, splattered them with spoiled cream. Dogs whined; people shrieked.

The only humans who escaped the insanity, from what Bromwyn could see, were those whose doors were protected by an iron horseshoe nailed over the entranceway. But far too many of the people of Loren didn't believe in the old stories. Those with horseshoes over their doorways probably had put them up to bring about good luck rather than to ward off attacks from storybook fairies.

Bromwyn snorted in disgust. She didn't know whether to pity the grownups or to be annoyed at them.

As they passed the bakery, Rusty halted.

Bromwyn skidded to a stop and turned to look back at him. He was gaping at the ruins of the front door, at the breads and pastries thrown to the ground, at the spilled flour matting the floor.

"I have to make sure my mam and da are all right," he shouted over the din.

Bromwyn opened her mouth, about to offer him words of comfort, but then she saw a huge gathering off to her left. "No time for that," she said to him, her voice strangled. "Look there!"

She pointed to the center of the main avenue, where children were lining up in the Village Circle like string toys. Dozens of boys and girls, most of whom were in their nightclothes, were listening to the fey speak to them. The fey's words would be sickeningly sweet, and their promises would be as beautiful, and as fleeting, as a rainbow. Once ensnared by such false promises, the children would happily follow them off a cliff, should the fey tell them to.

Rusty wailed, "But my parents!"

"Then look for them!" She whirled to face him, her hands out, placating. "But I cannot leave the young ones alone with the fey! You know what they will do to them!"

He glanced from the street to the bakery's smashed door, back to the children in the Village Circle. With a miserable look, he nodded at Bromwyn, and the two of them dashed up to where the children were gathered.

As they approached, Bromwyn heard, over the sounds of the screaming grownups and nervous animals and the chortling fey wreaking havoc, the not-Brends and not-Jalsas offering the children all sorts of wonders, should they just follow them through the World Door. Some of the youngsters were barely more than toddlers, and they held the hands of their older siblings or clutched onto their rag dolls, blinking away sleep as they tried to understand what was happening. Others were nearly as old as Bromwyn and Rusty, and though they had suspicious looks on their faces, many of them also had a hopeful sheen to their eyes.

Bromwyn looked about the Circle, hoping for some help. But it was painfully clear that she and Rusty were on their own. Insanity had gripped the village, and the adults, caught in their own terror and dismay, were ignoring the children. Or perhaps the fey had used their magic to make the children invisible to their parents, and the parents invisible to their children.

That had to be it, Bromwyn decided: No parent would willingly allow a child, any child, to go off with the fey. And most children wouldn't ignore watching their own parents suffer from magical stings and welts—at the very least, they would probably giggle.

"Yes," a Jalsa was saying to a group of younger children, lined up as neatly as Master Tiller's fields of spelt, "you may have sugar cookies to break your fast. Sugar cookies for lunch as well!"

"And even for dinner," said another Jalsa. "Sugar cookies forever and always!"

"But only in our land," said a third. "Only if you walk with us through the magic Door for no other reason than that you wish to join us in our land."

"Which, of course, you want to do," said a Brend with a wide grin.

"Of course," chorused all of the Jalsas.

"What're they doing?" Rusty whispered to Bromwyn.

She replied, "Cheating."

The fey weren't breaking the rule, because they weren't stealing the children. But they were very happy to lie and trick the children into going with them through the World Door. Or maybe there really would be sugar cookies for all meals. Anything could be possible in the land of the fey. How terribly unfair—Bromwyn had to compete against pastries.

The thought made her furious. Well and good; for what she planned on doing, she needed to be at her imposing best. She stepped forward.

"What about sticky buns?" asked a small girl, raising her hand politely.

"Whenever you wish!" declared all the Jalsas together, and a cheer went up among the children.

Bromwyn narrowed her eyes. "Children of Loren," she bellowed, mimicking her grandmother's and mother's disapproving tones to icy perfection. "What, pray tell, do you think you are doing?"

The children let out startled gasps. Hasty whispers of "Bromwyn Darkeyes!" and "Lady Witch!" buzzed among them, and Bromwyn, smiling grimly, did her best to look her worst.

The fey stared at her and smirked at her. Some openly mocked her.

Bromwyn noted that while the fey were all copies of Brend and Jalsa, none of them were exact copies; something about them was off, just a little bit: a mite too tall or too short, skin too clear or too ruddy, hair too curly or not long enough. It was just enough to show they were actors dressed for their roles, yet still quite overwhelming.

Or they would have been overwhelming, had Bromwyn not been as tired, and as furious, as she was. She pulled herself up straighter and lifted her chin.

One older boy shouted, "We're off to fairyland. And you can't stop us!"

A few of the other children weakly agreed. All of them stared at her, as if waiting to see what she would do.

The fey leered, and some began to insult her.

Bromwyn ignored the false Jalsas and Brends completely, acting as if they were beneath her notice. They couldn't harm her or Rusty directly; according to the village's law, they themselves were still children until their seventeenth birthdays, and so they could not be stolen or marked. The Allenswood attack had probably been meant to scare and delay them; it would have been simple for the enchanted wood to have trapped them and dragged them into the earth, where they would have suffocated. The very thought temporarily banished Bromwyn's exhaustion.

She arched an eyebrow and glared at the boy who'd shouted at her. "And what makes you think I would care to stop you, Jordan Rivers? If you want to throw away your life, all on the promise of sugar cookies, go right ahead."

"And sticky buns," a girl added, but someone shushed her.

"Go on," Bromwyn said. "Show the fey that you are as easily led as sheep to the slaughter."

Jordan looked like he was going to be sick.

"They're not going to kill us," one of the older girls shouted.

"They're going to feed us, and play with us!"

"Yes, yes," Bromwyn said dismissively. "I know what they said. I have heard their promises before." She stared hard at the girl. "They will feed you, until they forget you are human and need to eat more than once a fortnight. They will play with you, until they move onto other, shiner toys."

"The witchling sounds bitter," a Brend laughed. "It sounds like she was not invited to come play."

"She is jealous of you," a Jalsa crooned. "Jealous that she is not allowed to play in our land."

"We will always play with you," said another. "Always and forever."

"And you will never miss your boring home," said another Brend. "Never never."

"They are lying to you," Bromwyn said to the children. "You should know better, each and every one of you."

The older ones paled and looked away, but the younger ones—the ones who were not old enough to have heard that they were supposed to be afraid of Lady Witch—frowned at her.

"How do you know?" one little boy demanded.

"Because they are fey," she answered. "That is what they do. They lie."

"We never told you anything that you did not want to hear," a Brend said with a silky chuckle. "The witch just did not get what she wanted, so she is unhappy."

"And taking it out on you," another Brend said.

"She is being mean," said a Jalsa.

"And she does not want you to have any fun," said a second.

"None at all," said a third.

"Meanie," said all the Jalsas, and they stuck out their tongues at Bromwyn.

Bromwyn turned her scathing glare to the fey.

"Oh look," a Jalsa said with a huge grin. "We made her mad!"

"I bet she is going to cry," said a Brend.

"No bet," said all of the other Brends.

Some of the older children laughed.

Bromwyn narrowed her eyes. Without saying a word, she cast from the Way of Sight. As earlier, her closed hand shimmered and brightened until it glowed as if she held a star inside of it. But this time, there was a touch of heat to the glow, a hint of actual sunlight—which was as deadly to fey creatures as poison was to people.

Bromwyn had a moment of surprise, but she quickly tamped that down until it was nothing more than a wary buzz in the back of her mind. The heat must have been left over from when she had readily embraced Fire to battle the burning fields. Well and good; she would happily take all the help she could get.

The fey hissed, and many flinched from the shining light radiating from her hand. Some of the creatures growled, their false human mouths making sounds no human ever could.

The smaller children began to cry.

"Mind your tongue," Bromwyn said to the hissing fey. "And stop scaring the little ones. Some playmates you will be, terrifying the poor things like that."

"Go away!" the Jalsas yelled at her.

"You are no fun!" the Brends shouted.

The children looked uneasy, and some scampered to the back of the lines, but none of them turned away.

Bromwyn wanted to scream at them. The dumb bunnies! She should let them all go with the fey! They deserved each other!

"Come with us," one of the Jalsas said, "to a place where you will never be bullied by witches or grownups, ever."

"Come with us," one of the Brends said, "to a place where it will always be playtime."

All of the fey grinned, and there was nothing human about those grins. They all said, "Come with us."

And many of the children grinned back.

Just then, Rusty pushed his way in front of Bromwyn. "Now see here," he bellowed. "You kids hear me right now! If any of you go off with the fey, I'm going to tell on you!"

There was utter silence, save for the sound of grins sliding off of faces.

"I'll tell *all* of your parents just how naughty you are," he shouted, wagging a finger at the children of Loren. "How you cared more for *eating cookies* than you did for your mams and das! How you were ready to go off with *strangers!*"

Now the children squirmed.

"I'll get in so much trouble," one girl cried.

"You will!" Rusty agreed. "And it'll be all your fault!"

"Do not listen to him," said one of the Brends desperately. "Come with us! Play with us, forever!"

"And always," the Jalsas begged.

Rusty snorted. "I see you, Annie Smith and Catie Underhill. I see you, Liam Small and Hannah Goodwyn. I see *all* of you. And I promise you, your parents will know the truth." He crossed his arms and glowered at them. "See if any of you will be able to sit down when they're done spanking you! I bet your bottoms will be so sore, you'll stand for the better part of a month! And you'll deserve it, each and every one of you. Like Lady Witch said, *you know better.*"

The children shuffled their feet. And then Jordan Rivers said loudly, "I'm going home."

With that, the boys and girls of Loren slowly made their way back to their houses. Bromwyn didn't dare to release her breath until the last child began to walk back home.

After watching their prey leave, the fey turned to face Bromwyn and Rusty. They all looked angry, but some also looked scared.

"That was cruel," a Jalsa pouted.

"Mean," said another.

"Spoilsport!" shouted the Brends.

Bromwyn took all of them in with her dark gaze. Fury pounded through her, and when she spoke, her voice was a low rasp. "You will leave the children alone this night. All of them. You will not trick them, or beg them to leave the safety of their homes. And you will not trick them into letting you enter. Or else."

A Jalsa sneered at her. "Or else what?"

Bromwyn smiled then, a cruel smile that felt very right on her face. And then she raised her star-bright hand to point at the fey creature, channeling her magic to make the light shine as intensely as when the World Door had opened.

The Jalsa flinched, but she didn't turn away.

Still smiling, Bromwyn said, "Or else I will call down the power of the sun itself, and will remind you why the fey cannot remain in our land during the day."

The pretend Jalsa snarled at her, and showed far too many teeth. "Come," she said to her fellows, "the witchling is not worth our time." Then she flew away.

The other fey followed suit, and soon Bromwyn and Rusty were left alone on the main avenue of Loren.

She blew out a breath as she unraveled the spell. "That," she said, "went very well."

Rusty let out a shaky laugh. "See that? We can do this. No problem."

That was when they heard a piercing scream.

# KEEPING THEIR HEADS

"It's from over there," Rusty cried, grabbing her hand. "Come on!"

He and Bromwyn dashed down the street full-tilt, and Bromwyn would have stumbled more than once had Rusty not been holding onto her. Between the mud and the rotting fruit, the streets were slick; thanks to the smashed furniture and ruined goods scattered everywhere, the streets were dangerous, even without the taunting fey throwing things at them. Bare feet and long skirts, Bromwyn acknowledged, had their limitations after all.

Around them, madness ensued. Adults ran in circles, shrieking fit to tear the sky. Panicked livestock scampered about, screaming in their own ways. Chickens squawked and fluttered in the mud; pigs squealed and tramped over anything in their path. Bromwyn and Rusty ran on, careful to avoid wreckage and maneuver around stunned sheep (a number of which now sported bright orange wool). Two oxen lumbered out of their way, the ruins of their harness dangling by their sides. Bromwyn's nostrils stung from the acrid smells of burned grain and charred trees, as well as from the deeper, cloying stench of wet animals.

There was another screech, the sound terrified and desperate. Bromwyn yanked up her skirt and forced herself to run faster. Legs bare to her knees, she bolted forward with Rusty by her side, squeezing her other hand like a vise.

Over their heads, the fey capered and jeered. As she ran, Bromwyn felt something whirl past her cheek. Something else splattered against the back of her head, then dripped down her back.

"They say milk is good for the hair," an overly sweet female voice called out—close to Jalsa's, but pitched too high.

"But it tends to make witches age!" cried another. "Look how her face has already wrinkled!"

At that, Bromwyn cast an evil look over her shoulder. If she had walked the same Way of Witchcraft as her grandmother, the look truly would have killed.

"That is not aging—that is anger!" declared a third. "Look how ugly it makes her!"

The three false Jalsas tittered laughter.

Rusty pulled her along hard enough to nearly dislocate her shoulder, so she gave up on glaring and concentrated on keeping her footing. The mud squished beneath her as her feet slapped down. She and Rusty dashed through the main intersection, and she realized with dismay that they were heading toward the church.

In front of the church's wrought-iron gates, directly below two monstrous iron baskets filled with burning pine knots, a large crowd had formed. Bromwyn recognized most of the people, and it looked as if more than half of the village's adults had gathered there with rage on their faces and murder in their eyes. They all were shouting, and many had their fists pumping in the air. But Bromwyn couldn't understand a thing they were saying—it was all buzzing, like the rumble of a building thunderstorm.

She and Rusty pushed their way through until she was able to see, directly in front of the church gates, the four people who were facing the mob. She easily recognized Nick Ironside, the village's blacksmith. In his large hands, he gripped a huge axe.

Bromwyn's brow furrowed. Was he trying to incite the crowd to attack the fey?

Next to the blacksmith was the village's priest, looming like royalty for all of his plain brown robes. His arms were wide, as if he were appealing to the mob, but any words he spoke were lost in the crowd's roar. Instead of looking discomforted, as she would expect a man of the cloth to appear in the face of building violence, the priest seemed at ease, even confident.

The sight made Bromwyn's throat tighten, and she swallowed the lump that had formed there.

The other two people were on the ground: a man and a woman, lying prone, their arms pinned behind them in thick ropes. Bromwyn couldn't see their faces, but their clothing was filthy and torn. Before she could try to make sense of it all, the priest spoke.

"Yes," he shouted, and the crowd settled—but even that hush

was a thing of pending action, a palpable sense of something about to occur, of anticipation so thick that Bromwyn felt like she was choking. He declared, "This is all because of these two! What say you, people of Loren? Should they be brought to justice for all the damage they have wrought?"

"Yes!" bellowed the mob.

Bromwyn's body vibrated with the crowd's fury.

The woman cried out again, and the man looked up to glare at the priest. Bromwyn's heart dropped into her stomach as she recognized her husband-to-be. No fey copy was this one; this was her betrothed, filthy and bloody, with two blackened eyes and his hands bound cruelly behind him. Sprawled next to Brend, the blond woman sobbed again, her hands as tightly bound as his. It was the tavern maid, Jalsa, no longer looking so wantonly pretty. Her body trembled, and she begged to be released; she would do anything, she screamed, if only they would please, please let her go.

The priest smirked at her, but his words were to the crowd. "What say you, people of Loren? Do we let her free?"

"NO!" shouted the villagers, and Bromwyn flinched.

"Should she pay for her crimes?"

"YES!"

"I haven't done this thing," Jalsa cried, "I haven't, please, you must believe me!"

"Close your mouth!" Old Nick rasped, hefting his axe.

Bromwyn shouted, "NO!" She pushed her way forward until she was standing in front of Brend and Jalsa. She held her arms wide, as if she could protect them from the wrath of the blacksmith, from the crowd, from the fey circling over them. She cried out, "Are you people mad? Stop this!"

"Out of the way, girl," Old Nick growled at her, his knuckles whitening on the axe handle.

"Not until you see reason!"

Rusty joined Bromwyn in front of the church gates, squatting low to shield the terrified tavern girl. "They haven't done anything," Rusty snarled at the blacksmith. "Let them go!"

"The girl's in league with demons," the blacksmith said. "So's the boy."

Brend didn't rise to the bait, nor did he beg. Instead, he glared his fury at his master, and the hatred that radiated from him was hotter than the fire of his forge.

Bromwyn shouted, "You have lost your mind! All of you! These two are innocent! Brend works for you, Master Smith!"

"I trusted him like my own son." The blacksmith shook his head sadly and sighed. "Breaks my heart, but there's only one way to deal with the devil. And that's in blood."

Next to him, the priest grinned.

Rusty yelled, "You can't do this! I won't let you do this!"

"Derek Jonasson!" shouted a man's voice. "You get back here right now!"

Rusty blushed from forehead to chin, but he kept his head high as he turned to face the speaker. "Sorry, Da, but I can't do that. I won't let him kill Jalsa or Brend. It's not right."

"Master Smith," Bromwyn pleaded, "put down the axe."

The blacksmith gripped the handle tighter. "The boy's got the devil in him. So does the girl."

"They have no such thing!"

"The priest says it's true."

"He is *wrong*," Bromwyn insisted.

A man shoved his way to the front of the crowd. The mayor, wearing the remnants of his Midsummer finery, shouted, "Look around you!" He motioned to the village at large, where dozens of Brends flew through the air. "The smith's apprentice and the serving girl both, they caused the chaos here tonight! How else do you explain the demons flying about in their images?"

"They're no demons," Rusty shouted at him. "They're fairies!"

The mayor stared at Rusty for a moment, then threw back his head and laughed. "Hear that?" he said to the mob. "They're fairies!"

A bubble of laughter from the crowd, along with taunts to make even the fey take note.

Bromwyn bit her lip to keep from screaming at them all. That would do no good, and it would probably make everything worse.

"They are demons," the priest insisted, and once again the assembled grownups hushed. "That is why our church has been left untouched. They cannot stand the presence of our mighty god."

"What they cannot stand is the wrought-iron gate around the church," Bromwyn said.

The priest looked down his nose at her. "This from a witch," he sneered. "And not even a grown witch, at that. Who are you to question the power of our god? You, who have never set foot within the church?"

She felt her rage building once more, twisting her heart. The priest simpered at her, just for a moment, and then the look was gone—but not before it made Bromwyn pause.

"They are demons," he said louder, looking at the adults crowding around them. "And as is their way, they have taken the images of those who have summoned them! These two!" He motioned at the prostrate forms of Brend and Jalsa. "They are in league with the devil, and we must cut it out of them! Only that will save the village! Master Smith, you will fulfill your obligation as Village Justice and smite the evil from their bodies with a mighty blow of your axe!"

Bromwyn gaped at him. *This* was the man who was known far and wide to be mild, both in word and deed?

The mob shouted its approval of the priest's demand, but all Bromwyn could hear was Jalsa's tortured whimper—and all she could see was how the priest silently gloated. He was goading them on, inciting them to action. It was quite unlike a peace-loving priest.

"This is insanity," Bromwyn shouted. She turned to the mayor. "Stop this! Whatever you might think, they are still residents of Loren!"

"They forswore any allegiance to Loren when they bargained with the devil," the mayor decreed. "Their deaths will stop the demons and save the village!"

"Get out of the way, girl, lest you get hurt." The blacksmith's voice was gruff, and he raised his axe high, making ready to swing.

Bromwyn glared at the mob, at the faces of the adults of Loren, at the people who either feared her or were repulsed by her, as if she were a monster because of her ability to wield magic. They were so angry, so afraid, so horribly certain they understood the cause of their terror. They were so proud and so *wrong*. How could she get them to listen to reason?

"You can't kill them," Rusty cried. "You're making a mistake! It's not demons, I'm telling you! It's fairies!"

A pause, in which Bromwyn heard her own ragged breaths, her own heartbeat thumping wildly. And then once again, laughter rippled from the grownups—all save the priest, whose dark eyes glistened.

"Fairies," the priest repeated, turning the word into something distasteful. "You have been reading too many stories, boy. Now stand aside, and let the blacksmith dispense justice."

And like that, Bromwyn knew what to do.

Gritting her teeth, she cast her magic wide, throwing it deftly over the large group of adults standing around them outside of the church. Once her spell of Sound was in place, she spoke.

"You mock this boy for reading stories," she said, and her voice reverberated over the crowd as if the winds themselves had taken her words and blown them to everyone's ears. "And yet, it is you who have forgotten the old stories. The true stories." She stood taller and took a step forward. "You have forgotten what history has taught us."

They were all looking at her now, even the priest, and the blacksmith lowered his axe, though he still gripped it hard enough that his hands shook.

"This village sits near a World Door," Bromwyn said. "And once every year, the Door opens, and fey come through for one night. That time is Midsummer, and that time is now."

"A child's story," the priest declared.

Bromwyn ignored him. "Long ago, when this village first was built, there was only one person who was able to keep the fey in their place. That person was Loren."

Now the priest laughed. "She speaks nonsense."

Old Nick murmured, "Let her have her say."

Apparently, the blacksmith loved a good story. Well and good. "Loren was brave," Bromwyn said, her voice rising, "and pure, and true to the other villagers. It was Loren who saved the village back then, who was able to tame the fey and use words as weapons, as easily as could those creatures of magic. It was he who tricked the fey into agreeing to come through the Door only once each year, on Midsummer's night. And it was he who held the great Key that locked the Door behind the fey at dawn, to ensure they did not find some trick that would allow them to steal back before the year was up. Loren was the first Guardian of the fey, and because of that, the village was named in his honor."

The priest snorted. To the mob he said, "You cannot mean to listen to such things!"

But listen they did. Bromwyn's spell was strong, and her words were compelling. She said, "You have forgotten Loren. You have forgotten that the fey are real. You have forgotten that they can hurt you, and they long to steal what is most precious to you.

Where are your children tonight, people of Loren?"

A gasp went through the crowd.

"They are back in their beds, thanks to the quick thinking of this boy," Bromwyn said, motioning to Rusty, "who has not forgotten that the fey are real, and that they would do anything to steal human children."

The baker exclaimed, "Derek, is this true?"

Grimly, Rusty nodded.

"What can we do?" one woman called out.

"Look around you. The only homes and shops untouched are those with horseshoes over their doors, or iron gates around their premises. Iron," Bromwyn said. "The fey cannot stand the touch of iron, and they will avoid any place with iron over its doorway, or in its shop prominently. Carry a piece of iron on your person, and the fey will leave you untouched." She stared hard at the priest. "Is that not right?"

The priest said nothing, but his eyes sparkled with mirth.

A murmur rippled through the crowd. "I don't have horseshoes," a man yelled.

"The only iron I have is my fryer," a woman shouted.

"It does not have to be big," Bromwyn said, still glaring at the priest. "All you need is an iron nail in your pocket."

"There are nails a plenty at the forge," said Old Nick, turning to the crowd. "I'll give nails to those who need them, free of charge! Come with me, all in want of a bit of iron!"

Then, as if a spell had broken—which it did, for Bromwyn unraveled it—the adults made their way to the forge. Bromwyn didn't watch them go; she was too busy locking gazes with the priest of Loren. Peripherally, she saw Rusty take his knife from his boot and begin to saw through Jalsa's bonds.

With a soft chuckle, the figure in the brown robes said, "Well played, witchling."

She bowed her head, acknowledging the compliment. "Where is the good priest, my lord?"

"Winnie?" Rusty paused in his rescue. "What are you talking about?"

Still looking at the man towering over her, she replied, "This is the King of the fey."

Rusty swallowed loudly, then sawed all the harder.

The false priest's face pulled into a wide grin. "He is inside his church," the King said, "in his small chamber next to the alter room, sleeping the sleep of the righteous." He gestured to himself. "He was not using his form, so I borrowed it."

"Clever, my lord," she said, hoping to both praise and stall him. The longer he dallied with her, the less damage he would do in the village. "I must admit my surprise. I would have thought the gates around the church would have deterred one of the fair folk."

"For any other than myself or my lady Queen, that is indeed the case." His grin pulled into something wicked. "As long as I do not touch iron, it bothers me none. And as I will never touch it, it will never bother me."

"As you say, my lord," she said, inclining her head again.

"Now that this game is done, I must go find another before I grow bored." He motioned lazily. Overhead, the two streetlights went out. "Until the blue hour, witchling!"

Bromwyn felt the surge of wind that told her that the King of the fey had leapt into the nighttime sky.

"Well," she said in the darkness, "that was rather spiteful of him." She cast from Sight, using her magic to give the illusion of light on the extinguished lamps. In their iron baskets, the pine knots glowed brightly.

"They have a wicked sense of humor," Rusty said.

"If humor is what you want to call it." She watched the King join the other fey, and she realized with dismay that she, too, longed to fly away, to soar among the winds and chase after the birds. What stung more than the realization was the knowledge that if she had chosen differently five years ago, she would have flown every single day. Had she gone to live in the land of the fey, there would have been nothing she could not do.

Nothing, except choose whom to love with all of her heart.

But given that she had no choice in the matter anyway, she felt horribly cheated.

*I made the right choice*, she told herself angrily. *Doing the right thing should not weigh so heavily.*

From behind her came a breathy sob, and a woman asked, "Is it over?"

Forcing herself to smile, Bromwyn turned to face Jalsa, who was rubbing her battered wrists. "Your innocence has been accepted. You have nothing to fear from the villagers tonight. But," she added, "you may want to carry an iron nail on you."

"Winnie?" Rusty didn't look up as he worked on the ropes that pinned Brend's arms behind his broad back. "How did you know it wasn't the priest himself? It looked just like him."

"Not completely," she said, darting a glance at Brend—who was looking at her so curiously—before she turned away. "Too much hair. When the fey mimic bodies, they do not seem to get it exactly right."

At that moment, four Jalsas floated past them … and two of them were completely naked.

Behind Brend, Rusty mumbled something that sounded like, "Close enough."

Bromwyn restrained herself from rolling her eyes. She said, "More than the appearance, the attitude was completely wrong. The true priest is a man of peace. He would never have urged people to commit murder."

Jalsa—the real Jalsa—let out a wail, and she threw herself on Brend, whose bonds fell to the ground. She cried, "They were going to kill us! And we didn't do anything to deserve it! Oh, it was horrible! Horrible!"

"There there," Brend said awkwardly, putting his arm around her. "It's over now. You're all right."

"Hey," Rusty said, affronted.

"Oh, Sir Smith, I was so frightened!" Jalsa sobbed (prettily, Bromwyn noticed) and clutched Brend's shirt. "But you were so brave! So courageous! So strong!"

"So helpless," Rusty said.

Bromwyn didn't know whether she was terribly annoyed by her betrothed soothing the buxom barmaid or terribly amused.

"We were in dire straits for a time," Brend said, patting Jalsa's back as he continued to throw strange glances at Bromwyn. "But the good villagers saw the truth of things."

"You are right, Sir Smith," Jalsa said, looking up into Brend's dirty face. When the tavern girl spoke again, her voice was less tremulous and more of a throaty purr. "I feel the need to have something to drink, to soothe my nerves. But I am uneasy walking alone tonight. There are frightening things about. Would you accompany me?"

"I would be honored," Brend said gravely.

Bromwyn nearly gagged when Jalsa batted her eyelashes at him.

"This is so completely unfair," Rusty said to Bromwyn, who kept her mouth shut.

Brend held his arm out, and Jalsa took it. Together, they slowly walked away from the church gates, as copies of them fluttered about the sky. Before they turned the corner that would lead to the tavern, Brend looked over his shoulder and caught Bromwyn's gaze. Whatever he tried to say to her with his eyes, Bromwyn couldn't tell. And then, the two victims were gone.

"In the stories," Rusty said loudly, "the thief prince gets the girl."

"If you were a prince in real life," Bromwyn said, "you would have gotten Jalsa. Who, I cannot help but notice, has been reduced once again to a girl. I thought she was a woman?"

"A wench," he said, puffing out his chest. "She's a wench if there ever was one. Say, Winnie, I remember learning about our village's history."

She slid a glance at him. "Do you, now?"

"Mistress Teacher spent many an hour on that particular tale. And there's nothing it in about anyone named Loren."

Bromwyn felt a blush heat her cheeks. "Perhaps that is because I made that part up."

Rusty stared at her for a good five seconds before he burst out laughing.

"What?" Bromwyn said, sniffing. "What is so funny?"

He shook his head as he laughed, and Bromwyn sighed as she waited for the fit to pass.

Finally Rusty said around his snorts, "The Wise One of Loren is a liar. How do you not see the humor in that?"

"The Wise One," another voice replied, "knows when to tell people what they need to hear."

Bromwyn stiffened. Rusty, facing her, gulped loudly, and she watched the blood drain from his face.

Biting her lip, she said a hasty prayer to Nature. Then Bromwyn turned to face the wrathful gaze of her grandmother.

# WISE WORDS

"You have returned," Bromwyn said meekly.

"And you have a penchant for pointing out the obvious." Niove Whitehair glowered down at her, and Bromwyn cringed. The lanterns hanging overhead cast deep shadows on her grandmother's seamed face, and the whites of her eyes glowed with power. For her to display even a hint of her magic so openly meant that she was completely livid with Bromwyn. That didn't bode well.

"I would ask how everything goes," her grandmother said with a sniff, "but that is painfully apparent."

No, that didn't bode well at all.

Bromwyn bit her lip and looked down at her muddy feet. She wished she could just disappear—which, strictly speaking, she could, but her grandmother would easily see through the illusion. And that would put Niove in an even worse mood.

"Tell me this, Granddaughter: Are the fey bound by any rules this night? Or have you forgotten everything?"

Bromwyn whispered, "They cannot steal children, or lure adults." She coughed. "Or eat them."

After a long pause, Niove said, "Well then, that is something, at least. Still, I expected better from you." She snorted in disgust. "Look at them, romping about, frolicking as if this were their own personal playground. Makes me want to spit. You should have done better than this, girl."

Blushing furiously, Bromwyn said nothing. She was too upset to even be angry at her grandmother's words, for Niove was right. Bromwyn should have done better. And not because of the risk of losing her magic, but for the larger reason: The people of Loren were suffering for her oversight. She bit back a sob.

"Don't talk to her like that."

Bromwyn couldn't have heard properly. Surely, she imagined Rusty coming to her defense. No one, not anyone, ever talked back to Niove Whitehair.

Her grandmother boomed, "Who are you, boy, to tell me how I may speak to my granddaughter?"

*Fire and Air,* Bromwyn thought. *Rusty really did speak aloud!* She wanted to kiss him and curse him, but she couldn't bring herself to say or do anything, other than tremble before her grandmother and await judgment.

"I'm her friend," Rusty said, his voice steady and not sounding at all scared. "And more than that, I'm the Key Bearer. It was my idiocy that got us into this mess, not hers."

By Nature's grace, her best friend was possessed. That had to be it. There was no other explanation for him being so pert to the village Wise One, or why her grandmother hadn't stricken him down by now. Bromwyn's temper was short; Niove's was legendary.

"An honest thief," her grandmother mused. "Who would have guessed?"

"Bromwyn Darkeyes is the one who saved Master Tiller's fields," said Rusty, sounding not at all like the boy Bromwyn knew—he sounded older, more confident. "And she's the one who talked sense into the mudrats before they did something horrifically dumb, like follow the fairies up the Hill and through the Door. And she's the one who talked the village adults out of a murder or two."

"Really," Niove said thoughtfully.

Bromwyn felt her grandmother's gaze raking over her, and she desperately tried not to whimper. Witches never whimpered, not even when under the intense scrutiny of older, more terrifying witches.

"I'd say she's got much to be proud of," Rusty said, and now Bromwyn could hear a grin in his voice. "I'm proud of her. And I'm proud to call her my friend. That's who I am, Wise One: the friend of Bromwyn Darkeyes."

Then there was silence, thick as the baker's festival bread.

Bromwyn couldn't believe what Rusty had said, or that he had spoken at all. Talking back to Niove Whitehair? He must have gone mad indeed.

"Not many have the strength of character to speak their minds to me," Niove said slowly, approvingly. It was a tone that Bromwyn had rarely heard, and almost never when it came to Bromwyn herself. "My granddaughter is lucky to have you as a friend, boy."

"Thank you, Wise One."

"But it seems to me," she said, much sharper, "that your stint as Guardian is going less than well. Would you say that is accurate?"

"Yes, Wise One," Rusty said, his voice shrinking until his words were tiny things. "It certainly could be going better."

"And it could end up going significantly worse."

Bromwyn heard the threat in her grandmother's words, and she chewed her lip.

"Leave us, boy. Go to the cartomancer's shop, and wait there for my granddaughter. She and I must have words now."

"Yes, Wise One," he squeaked. "Thank you, Wise One."

Bromwyn heard him scamper away, leaving her to her fate. She couldn't blame him for running; when Niove said frog, you hopped. Very, very high. She swallowed, and waited, and wondered if her grandmother was going to kill her now, or wait until after Midsummer.

"I know of your words to the children of this village," Niove said once Rusty had gone. "Especially to that Jordan Rivers, who has not a lick of sense to him. I saw you hold your own in front of the mob, and speak to the fey King on his own terms. But I do not know what your thief friend meant by saying you saved Jason Deerborn's fields. Explain."

Doing her best not to stutter, and failing miserably, Bromwyn told her grandmother how she put out the fire in Master Tiller's spelt fields. She still couldn't bring herself to look Niove in the eye, so she addressed her own muddy toes.

When she finished, there was a long pause before her grandmother spoke, a pause filled with Bromwyn imagining the worst sorts of punishments Niove could dish out, many of which having to do with cleaning out the privy behind her grandmother's cottage.

"And so." Niove let out a sigh. "At least you did not burn yourself out. That counts."

Bromwyn said, "Rusty doused me in water … "

"I do not speak of your body, girl. Do not be daft; it ill-becomes you."

Bromwyn gleeped and bit her tongue. She had not considered that calling Fire and Air might well have destroyed her ability to cast. Had she known, would she still have taken the chance?

"Well," Niove huffed, "once this night is done and the World Door is closed, we will have much to discuss. Assuming, of course, the fey will not be returning for a year's time. They have not challenged you, I take it?"

Bromwyn whispered, "They did, Grandmother. They challenged Rusty for the right to walk the world every night this year."

"And you were going to tell me of this *when*, girl? After the King and Queen had enslaved the village? Wheel and want!" Niove spat loudly, and Bromwyn flinched. "Priorities, girl! You

157

need to learn priorities!"

"I am sorry," Bromwyn cried. "Truly! I was going to tell you. It is just … " She took a deep breath, and then she said, "I was afraid to."

"Why?"

Bromwyn admitted, "I thought you would kill me."

"And I still might."

Bromwyn screwed her eyes shut and tried not to die on the spot.

"Even so," her grandmother said, "your duty is first and foremost to this village. You are to be a Wise One. Or have you forgotten that?"

"No, Grandmother," she whispered.

"Stop putting yourself first, if you plan on ever filling my shoes. So to speak. Where in Nature's nurturing earth are your shoes? You met the fair folk *barefoot*?"

There was a sudden sting by Bromwyn's ear. "Ow!"

"Bromwyn Elmindrea Lucinda Moon," her grandmother hissed, "the next time you are to represent this village as a Wise One, you will dress appropriately! You are not some mudrat!" She clouted Bromwyn's other ear. "Do you hear me, girl?"

"Yes, Grandmother," she said, rubbing her sore ears.

Niove spat again. "So, the boy is to be challenged. Well, that is a complication." Then she let out a sigh, which to Bromwyn's stinging ears sounded almost mournful.

"But you will help us," she said to Niove, "now that you have returned. Right?"

"Of course not, girl," her grandmother said. "This is your test, and I will not interfere."

Niove's words made Bromwyn forget to be embarrassed or scared or ashamed, and she met her grandmother's dark gaze with her own. "What do you mean? You have to help us!"

"Perhaps your spell of Sound left some residual effects," Niove said dryly. "Are you deaf? I said I will not interfere, and that is what I meant."

Bromwyn spluttered, "But that is insane!"

"Call it what you want, girl." Her grandmother's eyes glowed fiercely, and her smile was a nightmare stitched onto her weathered face. "But I will not lift a finger to help you."

"Fire and Air!" Bromwyn stomped her foot, and mud splattered on her skirt. "You take me to task for daring to place my own needs above those of the village, and yet when I ask you for help for the good of the village, you tell me you will not because of my test!"

"Exactly."

"You are as selfish as you accuse me of being! You helped Mother eighteen years ago. She said so herself. It was your quick thinking, she said, that kept the fey from overrunning the village!"

"Your mother failed her test," Niove said, "and lost her magic. She needed my help."

The words hung in the air between them, and Bromwyn gasped as she understood the meaning behind them. She said, "But I—"

"Have not failed. Not yet, anyway," Niove added, "although the night is still young, and anything could happen, I suppose.

Do you want to fail?"

Bromwyn's mouth hung open, but since no words flew out, she quietly closed it and shook her head.

"Then do not. It really is as simple as that." Her grandmother arched a white brow. "Now that you are done lecturing me, Granddaughter, I will be off. If I know the fey, they will have made a mess of the Allenswood. I mean to make them clean up after themselves."

"Grandmother, I—" Bromwyn's voice cracked, and she had to take a gulping breath before she could continue. "I am sorry."

Niove snorted. "Apologies are as worthless as a hairpiece in a rainstorm. Do not apologize, girl. Pass your test. Show me that all the years you have spent studying with me have not been a waste of my time."

Feeling very small, Bromwyn replied, "Yes, Grandmother."

"Remember my advice to you, and you will be fine." Niove Whitehair's eyes shone, and for a moment, Bromwyn thought she saw something sparkling there beyond her grandmother's power, something that hinted of love and pride. Then the moment passed, and all that was left was the quiet glow of magic. "When is the challenge?"

"Just before dawn."

"The blue hour? Humph. So they mean to make it quick, before the sun's full light shines and roasts them where they stand." Niove snorted. "They underestimate you, Granddaughter."

"If you say so," Bromwyn whispered.

"I do. They are arrogant. Remember that." Her grandmother

scrutinized her. "I suggest you and the boy thief get some sleep. You look ready to drop, and if you plan on helping your friend with the challenge, you need your wits about you. The fey will do no great mischief, not this night at least. Not when they believe they may be returning every night for a year," she added with a sniff.

"But then we should study, see what we can anticipate—"

"It would be a waste of time. You cannot prepare for a fey challenge. All you can do is try to outthink them. And for that, girl, you need to be sharp. And that means you need your rest." Niove adjusted her black shawl, and then she turned away. "I suggest you set a cantrip to kick you out of bed ninety minutes before dawn. That will give you ample time to get the thief, and get yourselves to the Hill. And this time, girl, you had best dress appropriately. And for the love of Nature, wash those feet of yours." Grumbling, she added, "Seeing the fair folk *barefoot*. Fire and Air, the girl is as heartblind as her mother ever was."

"Grandmother?"

Niove glanced over her shoulder at Bromwyn.

"Thank you."

Her grandmother smiled tightly. "Do not thank me yet, girl. First pass your test. Then we shall have words about what it truly means to be a Wise One, among other things."

With that, Niove Whitehair walked up the street. One of the smaller fey dared to throw dirt at her, and Bromwyn watched first as the dirt slid off of Niove's form, leaving her grandmother untouched, and then as the fey's hair caught fire. The creature shrieked and zoomed away, leaving Niove to amble on, undisturbed.

"I will pass," Bromwyn said softly. "Mark me on that. I will pass, and will do you proud."

As she slowly made her way to her mother's shop to get Rusty, Bromwyn realized that she didn't know if she had made the promise to her grandmother or to herself.

# PART 4:

# THE CHALLENGE

# BONDS THAT WILL NOT BREAK

Bromwyn rubbed her eyes as she waited for Rusty to come out of the bakery. Above her, the fey buzzed like gnats and swooped through the pre-twilight sky, but they left her alone. They did not taunt her or goad her on, did not acknowledge her in any way, not even to squat over her like a bird taking aim. Perhaps the King had told them to leave her alone. Or perhaps the fey that had crossed her grandmother's path had served as fair warning. Bromwyn didn't know, and she didn't care. If the fey were giving her a wide berth, so much the better. She was too tired to properly growl at the creatures, anyway.

She'd gotten only a few hours of sleep, and now her eyes were burning and her mouth seemed fixed in a permanent yawn. Her mother had woken with her, and had drawn the water for Bromwyn's bath, and had picked out her garments—which, sadly, had included shoes. Niove must have had words with Jessamin when Bromwyn was sleeping; her mother had not cared one whit about Bromwyn's appearance yesterday, but this early morning, all Jessamin had been able to talk about was how Bromwyn would look the part of a Wise One. And her mother had hummed and laughed and smiled brightly as Bromwyn had bathed.

Just thinking about it now made Bromwyn gnash her teeth. In the face of her daughter possibly losing her magic, Jessamin had been happier than Bromwyn had seen her in a long, long time.

Then she rolled her eyes at her own foolishness. She knew that her mother was just being supportive, as a mother should be. And if she had taken pleasure out of helping her daughter dress, what of it?

For Jessamin clearly had enjoyed herself. Once Bromwyn had dressed, her mother had set about working her own sort of magic over her daughter's long hair. Now there were so many pins and combs and ... and *things* in her thick curly tresses that Bromwyn didn't know how she would ever brush them out. And her head felt like it weighed a ton. No wonder storybook ladies always walked with their heads held high; if they dared to look down, the weight of their hairdo would send them crashing to the floor.

And that was why, thirty minutes before dawn, Bromwyn, yawning hugely, wore a flowing blue gown that had fancy beadwork by the sleeves and hem, and her hair was wrapped around and around itself in complicated coils and held in place with elaborate combs and pins (and other things that, as far as Bromwyn was concerned, had no names other than "hair glue"). A silver girdle disguised how the dress bagged over her lanky frame, and it also managed to play up her bosom in a grownup manner. An *extremely* grownup manner. The very thought of it made her uneasy. Her hand fluttered over her chest, her long fingers covering the rather daring neckline.

Simply put, she felt very much like an idiot.

"You look beautiful," her mother had told her not even ten minutes ago, just before Bromwyn dashed out the door to go meet Rusty. "Much better than I ever did in that dress."

Bromwyn hated it. Blue reminded her of the fey King, and the material felt much too smooth and delicate for a proper dress.

"You can have it back, if you miss it," she had replied, scowling at her reflection in the mirror. Really, she looked so ... so *unlike* herself. The fey were going to mock her. And Rusty would kill himself with laughter when he saw her. Yes, he would die laughing, and she would die from embarrassment, and they would both save her grandmother the trouble of killing either of them.

"Not at all. It looks marvelous on you." Her mother had sighed happily, in the way that only mothers could do. "And the girdle flaunts your figure."

In reply, Bromwyn had yawned hugely, and was flummoxed when her cleavage nearly burst free from her dress. Covering the exposed top of her bosom with her hand, she said, "I look like I should be working in the tavern."

Jessamin had snorted, sounding in that moment exactly like Niove Whitehair. "You look nothing of the sort. Common girls work in taverns. You, my daughter, are far from common. And

167

today, you look like a princess." Her mother's hand had smoothed away an errant lock from Bromwyn's forehead. "You should fix your hair this way more often. Show off that beautiful face of yours."

"It took you twenty minutes just to brush out the curls. I would rather spend the time doing other things."

"Pish-tosh," her mother had replied. "A little time on your appearance should be as important to you as a little time on your studies."

That was truly ridiculous, but Bromwyn did not say so.

Jessamin had smiled, perhaps taking her daughter's silence as agreement. "I can only imagine what Brend would say, should he happen to see you looking so fetching."

And now, waiting outside of the bakery in the darkest time before the blue hour, Bromwyn wondered not about her future husband's reaction but about another boy's. A boy with red hair, and a quick smile, and eyes that danced with mischief. A boy with a penchant for trouble and for taking what didn't belong to him.

*Stop*, she told herself, but she couldn't. She didn't love Brend. She didn't want to marry him, or to be with him for the rest of her life. Not Brend, who called her magic "deviltry." Not Brend, who could barely stand to look at her. Not Brend, who was all too happy to go off with Jalsa to the tavern and yet couldn't manage to say even a "thank you" to Bromwyn for standing by him in the face of his looming execution.

She remembered how, years gone, Brend had first turned away from her once she was no longer merely the cartomancer's daughter but Lady Witch.

Her hands clenched into fists. Brend Underhill, apprentice blacksmith of Loren, was brawny and imposing, and he certainly would protect Bromwyn once they were wed; it was the duty of husbands to protect their wives, even as it was the duty of wives to side with their husbands, as Bromwyn herself had sided with Brend hours ago. But would Brend ever stand up to Niove Whitehair? Would he talk back to her grandmother and dare to tell her that he was proud of Bromwyn?

She could hear Rusty's words even now, could hear the grin in his voice as he told her grandmother that he was Bromwyn's friend.

Her eyes stung, and she blinked away sudden tears.

*Enough, and more than enough.* She sniffed loudly and brushed at her eyes. She didn't have the luxury of lamenting her life. Not now. Once she and Rusty met the King and Queen's challenge successfully and locked the World Door behind the fey, then she could lay about and mope and waste her time wishing for a rescue that would never come.

Besides, witches did not cry.

So it was a dry-eyed Bromwyn who met Rusty as he shuffled out of the bakery's storefront a few minutes later.

"Morning," he said around a jaw-cracking yawn—and then he froze, mid-yawn, and gaped at her.

If he laughed at her, she would die on the spot.

She forced herself to smile as she said, "Good morning." When a full minute went by without Rusty moving, she arched an eyebrow. "Is there a problem, Sir Baker?"

That made Rusty snap out of his stupor. Blinking, he lowered his hand away from his mouth. "No," he said, "no problem. Just a little stunned, that's all. You look … "

She lifted her chin and waited for the worst.

" … wow."

Hesitantly, she asked, "Is that a good wow, or a bad wow?"

"Good," he said, his voice cracking. After clearing his throat, he said again, "Good. Definitely good."

Bromwyn was thankful for the shadows cast by the suspended street lamps; otherwise, Rusty would have seen her blushing ferociously.

"But Winnie, what's with all … all this?" he asked, motioning to her from head to foot. "Look at that, Lady Witch is in shoes. I think I may have just died. Quick, pinch me."

"My grandmother's suggestion," she said, blowing out a sigh. At least the shoes were open-toed. Not barefoot, but close. And given the heat and the unseasonable dryness to the air this very early morning, last night's mud was now more akin to packed dirt, so Bromwyn's toes, while rather dusty, were not covered in muck. "Fire and Air," she muttered, looking at her toes, "that woman is going to be the death of me."

"I'm glad your granny didn't kill you."

"Yet," Bromwyn said. "What happens after dawn remains to be seen."

"There you go, getting all dour again." Rusty laughed, and Bromwyn couldn't help but watch how his eyes sparkled beneath his broad-brimmed hat and how his narrow shoulders bobbed in time to his mirth. "You'd think it was the end of the world."

She sniffed to show how serious she was. "It very well could be."

"To quote my favorite Lady Witch, 'what happens after dawn remains to be seen.' Say ... I should change into my best outfit, to be a better match for you. Otherwise they might mistake me for your footman."

"There is no time," she said. "We have barely a half hour before twilight."

"What, do you think I'm a *girl?* I can change my clothing in half a turn. Watch me."

"Rusty ... "

But he had already dashed back inside the bakery.

She growled, deep in her throat, then stomped her sandaled foot. Forget Niove Whitehair; *Rusty* was going to be the death of her. If she didn't kill him first.

\* \* \*

As it turned out, Rusty had been quite correct: It had taken him almost no time to change into his one suit. So, not even fifteen minutes later, Bromwyn and Rusty were already walking through the Allenswood, their path lit by the ball of light emanating from Bromwyn's hand.

Yawning, she led the way through the woods. As in the village, here the fey left them alone, choosing instead to flit through the trees and play tag in the deep grasses. Perhaps they had more interesting things to do in the last minutes before the blue hour than bother two humans making their way through the dark forest. Bromwyn thought briefly about gift horses and mouths, and walked on, turning over and over in her mind what the upcoming challenge could be and how Rusty could best it.

Rusty, who was whistling as he strode along with her. Rusty, who was smiling like he was on his way to yet another fine adventure. Rusty, who had all the brains of a milkmaid's stool. You'd think he'd be somewhat serious, considering how they were marching toward what could very well be the last day of their lives.

*Witches ponder,* Bromwyn decided, *and fools whistle.*

So she pondered. Too often, though, she caught herself stealing glances at her friend, who walked to her right. His dark brown wool coat and pants must have been horribly warm, but he didn't complain. She had to admit, silently, that the suit outlined his form quite nicely, even if the cut wasn't the finest. Bakers weren't butchers, after all, and though Rusty's family wasn't starving (which was hard to do when you baked for a living) Bromwyn knew they weren't able to afford the finer things. Thus, Rusty stole. Or tried to.

It was enough to make Bromwyn want to scream. Rusty could do anything he wanted to, anything at all. Why, he could even be a mayor or a manor lord, if he put his mind to it. She could picture him in his estate, a full-grown man with an entire village to look after. He would wear authority well. Much better than that floppy brown hat he so adored.

She frowned at him, not that he noticed; he was too busy whistling and prancing about, playing the part of the storybook rogue. Instead of planning for his future, he insisted on risking himself by following this idiotic fancy of being a thief prince. She had half a mind to scold him about it. At the very least, that would get him to stop whistling.

But they were not even five minutes away from the Hill, and perhaps ten minutes out from the challenge. Once they arrived, there would be little time for whistling or laughing or reassuring each other with quick smiles. So she allowed him to whistle as she fumed quietly over her friend's stupidity. He truly was a terrible thief. Assuming he survived the coming encounter with the fey, she had no doubt that one day Rusty would find himself in a very bad situation, one that Bromwyn wouldn't be able to help him out of. It would be such a shame if he lost those nimble-fingered hands of his, or worse, all because he picked the wrong pocket.

As her grandmother had said in her note, there were those who were not as lenient as she.

After a time, Rusty stopped whistling. Soon after that, he said, "You've been awfully silent."

Bromwyn, wrestling with the possibility of the fey challenging Rusty to leech himself without passing out from blood loss, or something equally barbaric, didn't respond. The fey did so enjoy blood. One of her mother's tomes that she had read included a handful of "human tales," which were stories told by the fey about unlucky humans who wound up on the other side of the World Door and the events that happened there. All of those stories were

173

bloody. Some of them, Bromwyn had been horrified to discover, had been recipes.

"Winnie?"

Bromwyn considered the possibility that the challenge would not involve blood, but water. Blood was thicker, but with the Loren River to the west of the village, water was far easier to come by. Unless, of course, the fey bled the villagers; they didn't have to steal children or lure adults, not if they were clever and merely wanted their blood. She remembered her grandmother's words, remembered Niove telling her that the King and Queen were arrogant. In their minds, they probably already saw themselves winning the challenge and returning to the Allenswood every night for a year—and what fun would that be if all of the humans were dead? They would have no playthings.

Rusty said, "What's the matter? Fairy got your tongue?"

She slid him a glance. The matter at hand was the upcoming challenge. And Rusty didn't seem to care one whit about it.

*Just look at him,* Bromwyn thought crossly, *practically sauntering in his one good suit, as if he were off to go courting.*

That made her think of the fey Queen's throaty laugh, and how she had touched Rusty's arm, and *that* made Bromwyn's stomach turn to ice.

Pushing aside thoughts of how the Queen had been flirting like a tavern girl—or, as Rusty would say, a tavern wench—Bromwyn said, "You know that human tongues are considered a delicacy among the fey, yes?"

"Yuck." Rusty twisted his face until it looked like he'd just

174

sucked a lemon. "That's rather nauseating. I'd say they have no sense of taste, but in this case, it's more like they have too much."

She rolled her eyes. No, clearly he wasn't worried about the challenge. At least *she* was trying to think things through. She muffled another yawn with her hand.

Rusty let out a dramatic sigh. "Bad enough you don't laugh at my jokes. Now they're boring you. I'm wounded, Winnie."

"I laugh when they are funny," she said absently, wondering whether the fey would issue a challenge that was entertaining, or demanding, or both, or neither.

"Wounded, I tell you! To the soul!"

She ignored him. Something involving trickery, Bromwyn decided. Yes, it would have to be something along those lines. The fey enjoyed playing pranks even more than they enjoyed blood. Would they use their magic? Would that be unfair? Did the fey care about such trivial things as fair and unfair?

Rusty harrumphed. "I'm practically bleeding here from how you've cut me."

Bromwyn's head started to throb, and she rubbed her temple with her non-spelled hand. Fire and Air, the challenge could be *anything.*

"Ruthlessly cut me! Completely lacking in ruth!"

Sighing, she began to see the wisdom in her grandmother's suggestion that she not waste time wondering what the challenge could be. She hated it when her grandmother was right.

*All you can do is try to outthink them,* Niove had said.

Well and good, but how were a witch and a so-called thief

supposed to outthink the King and Queen of the fey?

"See, now you look like you've swallowed a toad."

She shot Rusty a filthy look.

"An ugly toad," he said sweetly. "With warts."

"We are about to meet the fey," she said, her voice clipped and brimming with tension, "and they are going to challenge you for the right to walk the world for the next year. If we lose," she said, louder now, "Loren will be overrun. Children will be taken. Grownups will be eaten." And now she was shouting: "And to top it all off, if my grandmother does not literally kill me, I will surely lose my magic!"

"Oh, right," Rusty said, slapping his forehead. "That would be why we're walking in the Allenswood before dawn. And here I thought maybe we were stealing away to do something altogether inappropriate, like climbing trees while in our finest."

She growled, "How can you be making jokes?"

He looked at her, and she saw something desperate shining in his eyes. "Because if I don't joke, I'll scream. And that would be completely unmanly. So I'll joke about it, thank you very much."

She relented, and offered him a smile by way of apology.

He tipped his hat in acknowledgment and returned the smile.

They walked the rest of the way with Rusty whistling a jaunty tune. This time, Bromwyn hummed along.

Even before they came to the break in the woods that announced the glade with the Hill, Bromwyn saw bursts of light from the World Door shining through the foliage. She and Rusty walked past the shrubs that marked the boundary of the clearing, and there stood the Hill, with its circle of flat stones and the open Door glowing with trapped stars. None of the fey had arrived yet, from what Bromwyn could see, and that was fine with her. They had perhaps five minutes before twilight would be upon them.

Bromwyn's stomach lurched. Pressing her non-glowing hand to her belly, she commanded herself to remain calm.

*All will be well,* she told herself. *Rusty will pass the challenge, I will pass my test, the fey will go home, and we will return to Loren untouched.*

Closing her eyes, she slowly unraveled the spell of Sight, breaking down the magic that had made her right hand as bright as a lantern and then dispersing it into the air. Once that was done, she opened her eyes to find Rusty staring at his own hand.

Lying in his open palm, the Key winked with the lights of the World Door.

"All this trouble," he said. "All this hassle. All this nightmare, because of this small thing."

"I always thought the World Key should be bigger," Bromwyn said, glancing about to see if the fey were coming. Overhead, the sky was hinting at purple, dreaming of pink, and blackness was giving way to blue. Twilight was fast approaching.

"I caused all of this."

"Well, yes," Bromwyn said, peering at the sky. "But my grandmother started it. She wanted this to happen."

"Want." He laughed then, a dark and bitter sound that made Bromwyn look at him. He was still staring at the Key, and his mouth was stretched into a parody of a grin. "Must be nice, wanting something to happen, and then getting it."

She didn't like what she heard in his voice. "Rusty … "

"Want to know what *I* want, Winnie? I'll tell you. I want to be more than the baker's son. I want my life to mean more than punching dough and bartering over the price of grain. I want to run far away from Loren and never look back." He closed his fist over the Key. "I want to tell the woman I love that I love her," he said softly, "and I want her to run away with me so that we can spend our lives together."

Her throat tight, she said, "You love Jalsa now? And here I thought it was just a passing fancy."

"Not Jalsa." He looked over at her, his eyes shining brightly. "You."

All the air rushed out of her, and her heart pounded so hard that she thought it would break free from her body.

She squeaked, "Me?"

"I might die here," he said, his voice low. "Or wind up horribly disfigured on a permanent basis, or magicked into a tree, or something else altogether unappealing. But if I don't—if I survive this unscathed—run away with me."

"I cannot," she said miserably. "I have been promised to Brend."

"To that ungrateful lummox of a blacksmith's apprentice," he growled, "to become a Wise One to a village that doesn't appreciate you. Do you really long to be Mistress Smith?"

"You know that I don't," she whispered.

"So run away with me."

"I cannot," she repeated, feeling utterly wretched. "We have responsibilities. We cannot change that. I am bound to marry Brend, even as you are bound to the Key. We made our promises."

"Or they were made for us."

"It matters not; the results are the same."

There was a pause, laced with unspoken rage. Then Rusty said, "Some promises are meant to be broken." He pivoted and cocked back his arm, and then with a cry to shake the trees, he pitched the Key away.

"Rusty!" she shrieked, watching the Key arc up, then fall down to land just on the other side of the Hill. At least he hadn't thrown it through the World Door. "Are you mad?"

"Not hardly. I'm thinking clearly for the first time. Run away with me."

She whirled to face him. "You idiot, we have to get the Key back!"

"No we don't." He grabbed her hands, then dropped down to one knee. "Winnie, marry me."

"What is the matter with you?" She yanked her hands away. "We need the Key to lock the World Door!"

"Who cares about that? I'm talking about us."

"Rusty, stop being a fool! This is not the time! Please, I beg you, go get the Key!"

"No."

She wailed, "What do you mean, no?"

He pulled himself to his feet, and then he brushed off the soil from his knee. "I mean no."

With a furious screech, she ran over to where he had thrown

the Key and scooped it up. It was surprisingly light for such a weighty item; something as powerful as the World Key should at least take two hands to hold. So much trouble, as Rusty had said, caused by something that looked so common. It just proved you could not judge a key by its teeth—chances were it had the sort that bit you when you weren't looking.

Gripping the Key tightly, she dashed back to where Rusty stood, watching her. "Here," she said, offering it to him.

"No thank you," he replied, brushing off his cuffs. "It'll make my pocket bulge. Very unseemly."

She stared at him for a long moment, wondering if he truly had lost his mind. "We do not have time for your tantrum."

"Tantrum?" He chuckled, but there was nothing humorous about it. It was a desperate sound. "This isn't a tantrum."

She shoved out her hand. "Will you take the thing already?"

"No."

"Rusty, come on!"

"You just took it, so if you ask me, that makes you the new Guardian."

"Ooooh!" She stamped her foot. "You are impossible!"

"No, just insistent."

"Take it back!"

"Too late. I've given it to you. It's yours, Lady Guardian."

Her mind whirling, her heart breaking, she cried, "Why are you doing this?"

"To shock you awake." His face softened, and he said, "Winnie, you can do anything you want. You're strong and powerful and smart. If you don't want to marry Brend, then don't."

"I do not have a choice!" She meant to shout it to the winds, but her words were the barest of whispers.

"But you do." Softly, his voice as tender as a kiss, he said, "Come with me, today. Let's run away from all of this. Let's go somewhere else and start over."

"Running away is not the answer."

"Then what is?"

Bromwyn bit her lip, and stared at Rusty, at the boy—no, at the man—who had defended her when her grandmother berated her and who had stood by her side even in the midst of madness, who always made her laugh and feel not like some monster who worked with something dangerous but like a normal girl, someone who wanted to be and was meant to be loved.

She opened her mouth, and if things had been different, she might have agreed to run away with him and never look back.

But that was when the first blues of twilight illuminated the sky, and the sound of fey laughter froze Bromwyn's blood.

The blue hour had finally come.

# INSULTS

The first group of fey burst through the trees, dozens of them, screaming their laughter and buzzing like possessed bees. No longer in their Brend and Jalsa costumes, they were back in pretend-human blond-haired guises, androgynous and fetching, save for the hungry looks on their eager faces.

Bromwyn's fingers closed over the Key, and she shoved it into the pocket of her gown just before the fey swarmed around her and Rusty, darting near her face and hair, mocking them and jeering at them.

"The challenge!" one of the fey shouted happily.

Bromwyn blew out a nervous breath. At least the fey had not seen that Rusty had given up the Key; that would have been extremely bad. Bromwyn knew enough of fey etiquette to understand that for the Key Bearer to relinquish the symbol of office while he was officially acting as the Guardian would have been a grave insult to the King and Queen. And if one wished to survive an encounter with the fey, one absolutely, positively did not insult them. At least, not to their faces.

"The challenge!" the fey shouted, their voices filling the clearing even as more of their brethren joined them. "The challenge!" Fists pumped, they screamed their demand and their delight, with bloodlust in their eyes and saliva glistening on their lips. Still more of them arrived, hundreds now, adding their voices and banging drums, their words and music blending into a thrumming beat that screamed violence. "The challenge!" they chanted, they sang, they whooped like a battle cry. "The *challenge!*"

Bromwyn and Rusty stared at each other, wide-eyed, trapped in a crystalline moment of pure terror.

*Please*, Bromwyn thought desperately, calling out to Nature. *Stay with us. Guide us. Help us. Help him*, she prayed, thinking of Rusty and hoping against hope that he would manage to walk away from this with his mind, body, and soul unscathed.

To help give him strength, she looked deep into Rusty's eyes and said, "We can do this." Her words and tone made her sound far more confident than she actually felt, and for that reason, she smiled.

"We can," Rusty said.

And then he kissed her.

It was a moment that stretched on forever, and though the kiss was just a soft pressing of his lips upon hers, with only the faintest hint of a far deeper passion, to Bromwyn it was more powerful than even the strongest magic. It was perfect.

Too soon, far too soon, he pulled away.

Bromwyn's mouth tingled from his touch, and she thought she still tasted him on her lips. Rusty stroked her cheek, and she leaned into his touch.

He whispered, "For luck."

"For luck," she agreed, her voice breathy. She would have agreed to anything at that moment. She would have done anything for him. She would have given him the world. Around them, the fey shrieked and whooped, but Bromwyn no longer cared. Rusty was right there, smiling at her, and they were together. And that was all that mattered.

But then his gaze left hers to dart upward, and he froze. The smile slid off of his face, and Bromwyn saw him take a deep breath, and then another. They were frightened breaths, the sort one took to keep from screaming.

The King and Queen were coming.

Bromwyn sensed them before she saw them; a cold feeling of utter terror that stole her breath and made her head swim. Swallowing the lump in her throat, she looked up to see two bright dots, like fireflies alight, soaring through the air high above her. Their brightness sliced through the royal blue of the sky as if they fought the impending arrival of the sun.

Around Bromwyn, the fey horde shrieked and capered about, screaming their glee as their sovereign rulers descended. She ignored them as she watched the King and Queen dance in the air. As she did yesterday, Bromwyn again felt a stab of jealousy in her gut. The thought of flying away, of having the freedom to soar through the sky and tickle the treetops, was enough to make her grind her teeth. How she wanted to dance in the breeze, to forget the promises made by others that she herself had to keep, and just go wherever the wind took her.

How she wanted to be free.

*I want to tell the woman I love that I love her,* Rusty had said, *and I want her to run away with me so that we can spend our lives together.*

Could she do that? If she and Rusty survived the challenge, could she walk (not fly, no, never fly) away from her responsibilities, from her life, and start afresh with him by her side? Could she be something more than Mistress Smith, something other than the next Wise One of Loren?

Could she turn her back on everything she knew, all for the sake of one boy?

Watching the fey sovereigns slowly approach—still dancing and laughing, celebrating their final minutes before the dawn claimed the sky—Bromwyn bit back a sob. Bleakness shrouded her heart, so much darker than resentment, so much sharper than bitterness. So much colder than fear. It was a suffocating thing, a despair so thick that she couldn't breathe, couldn't think, couldn't do anything other than watch the King and Queen float down to meet them.

She didn't want to be here. But she had no choice; she couldn't let Rusty face them alone.

She never had a choice.

Now anger churned quietly through her, absorbing the bleak chill and slowly setting her blood to boil. This was her curse, her own personal doom, brought about not by her grandmother's magic, or even by Bromwyn's own hasty words, but by promises and power. To be a Wise One meant never being free to live her own life, never to dance carelessly until she was too dizzy to stand. Never to be with the one who loved her for herself. Never able to choose anything without giving thought to what others needed first. Bromwyn understood, right then and there, that no matter how her grandmother had framed the words, Bromwyn's was a curse that could never be broken.

She clenched her fists. *Is it so much for me to want something for* me? *Not Bromwyn Darkeyes, granddaughter of Niove Whitehair; not Bromwyn Moon, the cartomancer's daughter, but me?*

All of these feelings and thoughts assaulted her in less than four heartbeats, and she rode the emotions, allowed herself her resentment.

Then she shed her tumultuous feelings like snakeskin. She was Bromwyn, called Darkeyes, and she stood proudly as the magic of Nature resonated through her. Stone settled around her heart. Holding her chin high, she waited for the worst as the King and Queen landed in front of her.

The lord of the fey smiled at her and Rusty, a dark smile full of hidden meaning, and Bromwyn caught his scent: a heady aroma that made her think of spring rain on grass, of flowers blooming, of wild things doing what wild things did. Next to him, his lady laughed, a merry sound like wind chimes tinkling, and Bromwyn smelled honeysuckle—sweetness, like nectar and berries, with an underlying scent of something far sweeter, far wilder. The aromas mixed and caressed her like the most tantalizing perfume, making her feel giddy.

She bit the inside of her cheek.

With the sudden flare of pain, the smells diminished until they were just scents on the wind, enticing without being intoxicating. Though Bromwyn kept her stoic expression, her heart hammered in her chest and she barely restrained a shiver. Even now, just standing there plainly, the King and Queen called to her. And part of her longed to respond.

*I am no fey creature,* Bromwyn told herself. Her face was utterly calm, and it gave away none of her internal struggle. *I am a witch, a human witch, and I will not be swayed by fey magic.*

Her determination gave her the strength she needed: The longing dissipated, and she quashed the mad urge to dance before the King and Queen.

"Greetings to our host," the King said to Rusty, his voice echoing in the glade. He slid his gaze to Bromwyn. "And to his loyal and faithful companion."

He was calling her a *dog,* right there, to her face. Last night, she had been overwhelmed when the fey had insulted her so. Now, at this moment, fury seared her, white hot and insistent. Bromwyn pressed her lips together tightly and said nothing as she raged.

The King's grin pulled into something wicked. He'd noticed her reaction, and even now was all but laughing at her.

Rusty, either oblivious or intent on moving forward, swept off his hat and bowed low. It was picture perfect, right out of a storybook.

Bromwyn quickly followed suit and curtsied deeply. It wasn't as smooth as Rusty's bow, but at least it gave her an excuse to break eye contact.

"Greetings to the lord and lady of the fey," Rusty said. "Welcome back to the Allenswood."

"And to the World Door," added Bromwyn, still curtseying.

"You are prompt," said the King. "Here it is, the blue hour, and you are before my lady Queen and me, awaiting your challenge. How refreshing that we did not have to hunt you down."

"Like a cur," the Queen said sweetly, smiling at Bromwyn.

"And you are dressed appropriately!" said the King, motioning toward Rusty. "A little short in the sleeve and tattered by the ankle, but for a man-child, it is acceptable."

"He does clean up nicely," the Queen murmured, eyeing Rusty with clear appreciation. She was looking at him as if she wanted to savor him, feast on him … and not in a culinary way.

Bromwyn wanted to rip the Queen's eyes out.

"Such a pretty boy," said the Queen. "Yes, I would have the perfect place for him in my Court."

"My lady wife," said the King with a chuckle, "how many pages do you need?"

"As many as suits me." The Queen's words were light and yet sharp, like a blade so honed that you didn't feel it slice you, and Bromwyn wondered whether there was some anger between husband and wife. But then the Queen turned her gaze to Bromwyn. "And look at the witch girl, playing at being a lady."

Bromwyn blushed, but she held her curtsy.

"Indeed," the King purred, and Bromwyn felt his gaze sweep over her. "She looks like her mother."

Holding her skirt wide, Bromwyn's fingers clenched.

"Her mother?" The Queen pealed laughter. "I think the witch girl looks too innocent to be of her mother's blood. Her dress is baggy where her mother's was tight, and she is untouched where her mother was far too accessible."

Bromwyn's head snapped up, and her vision narrowed into a circle of red as she glared at the Queen.

"Still, she favors her." The King chuckled once again—a low, warm sound that made Bromwyn think of hungry monsters with very sharp teeth. "Her mother was far prettier, though. And much less restrained."

"For all the good either did her." The Queen smiled, her lips shining by the starlight of the World Door. "She lost her magic that very night, among other things. Remember, dearest?"

"I do. Like mother … "

" … like daughter."

Bromwyn's head pounded as she fought to control her temper. She had to keep her wits about her. She couldn't risk losing everything in a bout of hasty words and an ill-timed curse.

"Yes," the King said, his smile showing far too many teeth. "So very alike."

"Do you think that she will follow in her mother's footsteps?" the Queen asked idly.

The King's eyes gleamed. "That remains to be seen."

"Strange," Bromwyn said, no longer curtseying. "Here I thought that we were gathered to be challenged, not to make allusions to my mother's character. I had heard that the fey were better mannered than this."

The Queen's eyes narrowed dangerously.

"What Lady Witch means to say," Rusty said quickly, "is that time grows short, and unless the fair folk mean to extend their nighttime visit into daytime hours, we should get on with the business at hand. Right, Lady Witch?" He shot Bromwyn a look that was half-pleading, half-fury.

"Yes." Bromwyn blew out a calming breath, and then she fixed a bland smile on her face. "Please accept my apology for my hasty words." *And please,* she begged silently, *let my curse remain quiet.*

"You were rude," said the Queen.

Bromwyn inclined her head. "To my deepest regret."

"So you will forfeit a year of your life for your transgression."

She blanched. "My lady—"

Rusty cleared his throat. "I'm afraid, majesty, that Lady Witch is unable to meet your most reasonable request. In our land, she is still considered a child, and as such, she is in no position to offer any of her life to the fair folk. You see, because she is a child, her life belongs to her mother, rather like a favorite garment. And human women get so finicky about their possessions."

Bromwyn glared at Rusty, who completely ignored her. She turned back to face the fey rulers, deciding that when this was all done, she'd kill Rusty. Slowly.

The Queen cocked her head as she appraised Rusty, a bemused smile on her face. "And if I wait until she is no longer considered a child, my lord Guardian?"

"Then her life will belong to her lord husband," Rusty said, most apologetically. "You would have to ask him. But given his selfish worldview, I don't think he would be willing to release his lady wife to your good graces. He's a moron, you see."

The Queen laughed, and even clapped her hands in delight. "Well spoken, my lord Guardian! I accept the witchling's apology as it stands, with no other recourse."

Rusty bowed. "Your majesty's kindness knows no end. Thank you."

Bromwyn grated out her thanks as well, which the Queen completely ignored. She was too busy making eyes at Rusty. The Queen smiled mischievously, and her gown of flowers shifted— and suddenly the lady of the fey was as exposed as any tavern wench, the top of her bosom heaving as she purred, "You are quite the charmer, my lord Guardian."

"I thank you, my lady," Rusty said to the Queen's chest. "But I do not hold a candle to your own charms."

Yes, Bromwyn would kill him. Or better, she would have her grandmother kill him, then resurrect him, and *then* Bromwyn would kill him.

"You would make a most handsome page," the Queen murmured, sounding demure and yet completely wanton. "I offer this to you as a gift. Come with us through the World Door before the sun rises completely. You would be most happy in our land, Key Bearer."

"I am sure I would," Rusty replied smoothly. "But I am afraid I am bound to Loren. I am the only child to my parents, and as such, I must help them earn their lot in life. It is a son's duty, and I cannot ignore that commitment, not even to know the delights of your land. Though it pains me greatly, I must refuse."

*Oh, no.* Bromwyn opened her mouth to interject, but the Queen was faster.

"Well and good." The Queen's voice was lighthearted, and her smile was wicked, and Bromwyn understood that Rusty had made a grave mistake. "But if you lose the challenge, you lose your choice in the matter as well. Understand this, Key Bearer: Should you fail in your challenge, you will join us in our land."

Sweat popped on Rusty's brow. A nervous grin on his face, he said, "How's that now?"

"Well played, my lady wife," said the King, applauding.

Bromwyn felt like she would faint or throw up. Rusty had refused a fey gift flatly, instead of offering something of equal or better value.

"My lady," she said, "forgive my ignorance, for I am just a girl, and not schooled in the ways of the world. But it was my understanding that the challenge is for the right to keep the World Door open for a year's time, with no mention of the Guardian at all."

"It was," the Queen said, all traces of amusement gone. Her voice was regal, and altogether cold. "But that was before the Key Bearer insulted me by not accepting my most gracious gift. Now the challenge is both for the right to leave the World Door unlocked for one year, as well as for the right to claim the Key Bearer's soul. Or," she said, smiling a chilling smile, "if this does not please you, our two peoples can go to war."

# CHALLENGED

"This," Rusty said, "is really bad."

The King's eyes sparkled mischievously. "Are you suggesting that living in our world is unappealing?"

"No, my lord," Rusty stammered. "Not at all. It's just that my mam and da, see, they'll never understand how their only child went to live with the fairies."

The Queen's eyes darkened, and the King's face tightened.

"Which is how the common folk of our village refer to fair folk," Bromwyn threw in, desperate to save the situation from getting any worse. Calling the fey "fairies" to their faces—Nature have mercy! Her head was spinning, and her palms had begun to sweat. She had known that Rusty's life, and her own, would be on the line while entertaining the fey, but in her heart of hearts, she hadn't really thought it would come down to this. Now Rusty had

194

to meet the challenge successfully not just for the good of Loren but also for his own soul.

They had to best the fey.

"Well and good." The King clapped his hands once, and the sound thundered through the clearing. "The sun moves ever skyward, and our time here grows short. Let us begin the challenge."

Bromwyn waited for the executioner's axe to fall.

"You have proven yourself to be a smooth talker," said the Queen to Rusty, "one who knows the value of flattery. But have you learned to appreciate the value of truth?"

"Can you see what is plain before you?" asked the King.

"Or," said the Queen, "are you fooled by illusions that are more appealing?"

"And so, Key Bearer," the King said, "your challenge will be one of Sight."

Sight. Bromwyn knew Sight. She had an intimate understanding of it.

"My lord and lady," she said breathlessly, "I wish to take the challenge!"

An excited buzz resonated around her as the fey horde repeated her declaration to one another. Through hints of spring rain and honeysuckle, Bromwyn thought she smelled something else wafting from the King and Queen: anticipation.

The Queen arched an amused brow at her, but the King was looking at Bromwyn with something close to appreciation.

"Winnie," Rusty hissed in her ear, "are you mad?"

She shook her head. She couldn't tell him, not with the King and Queen staring at her so, but she would do anything to keep him out of harm's way. So she would take the challenge in his place. This was her test, and it was one of Sight. And she would not only rise to the challenge—she would pass her test, and keep her magic, and save both her friend and her village.

She could do it. Especially with Rusty right there, she could do it. She was his Lady Witch.

The King raised his arms, and the attending fey fell silent. "Agreed," he declared. "Bromwyn Darkeyes shall take the challenge."

Around them, the fey roared their approval.

"Majesties, I must object," Rusty spluttered over the cheering fey. "Clearly, Lady Witch has lost her mind. I think it's the lack of sleep, myself. A growing girl like her needs her rest. So I most respectfully beg you to reconsider her insane request and allow me to take the challenge as originally intended."

The fey quieted, save for a few isolated huzzahs.

The Queen said, "But my lord Guardian, we have already accepted the witch girl's most entertaining offer. What sort of visitors would we be if we refused such a gift after we had already accepted it?"

"Poor ones indeed," the King replied with a grin.

"So with all due respect," the Queen said, with just a hint of mockery, "we regretfully cannot grant your request. Which, truly, was moot before you even asked it."

"So we do not need to make a counteroffer," said her husband.

"The blue hour has begun. Let us discuss the terms of the challenge, as dictated by the challengers."

"A test of Sight," said the Queen. "To see the truth amidst the illusion."

"A test of Sight." The King nodded to Rusty. "With no help from the Key Bearer."

"None at all," said the Queen.

It hadn't occurred to Bromwyn to request any help, so she nodded her agreement. "A test of Sight," she said, "with no help from the Key Bearer. Agreed."

"Nice to be needed," Rusty muttered, crossing his arms.

Bromwyn ignored him. Let him be annoyed with her. Let him be angry with her. As long as he didn't take the challenge, there was a better chance that he would be safe. She lifted her chin, and she allowed herself a tiny smile. Rusty would be all right. She was a witch of the Way of Sight; this would be a challenge of Sight. How difficult could it truly be?

"A test of Sight," said the Queen, "in the allotted time."

"You must give your answer before twilight breaks into sunrise this morning," said the King, "lest you forfeit the challenge."

"And should you forfeit or lose the challenge, the World Door remains open," the Queen said with a toothy smile, "and the Key Bearer belongs to me. To us," she amended, sliding a glance at the King.

"Urk," said Rusty, looking distinctly pale.

"As my lady wife says." The King's smile was fierce, and his eyes sparkled with hidden thoughts.

Bromwyn nodded. "Agreed."

"And," the King said, "Bromwyn Darkeyes shall not use her magic during the challenge."

*What?* Flustered, hoping she had misheard, Bromwyn stammered, "But my lord—"

"No," said the King, raising a finger. "The time to make your requirements known was when you announced your intention to take the challenge. That time has passed."

"And only the challenger's requirements may be stated," added the Queen.

"And agreed to," said the King.

The Queen grinned, her teeth gleaming like knives. "Unless you wish to concede our victory."

"I," Bromwyn said, her mouth gaping. "I. I did not know … "

The King smiled lazily, like a wild beast contemplating which deer to eat first. "And what difference does that make, witchling?"

"None at all," Bromwyn said, feeling very, very small. Hadn't she just said the same thing to Rusty only yesterday? "Very well. I will not use my magic during the challenge."

"Winnie," Rusty hissed, "this is looking distinctly not in our favor."

"No," she agreed somberly. "It is not."

The King waved his arm, and Rusty let out a surprised yelp as his feet left the ground. Bromwyn watched in dismay as her friend rose in the air until he was hovering near the top of the World Door.

"My children," shouted the King, "look you well. Now clothe yourselves!"

With the King's command, all of the fey—the hundreds of blond-haired, blue-eyed, flower-garmented creatures of all sizes—now looked like Rusty, down to his floppy brown hat and threadbare suit. Many of the fey laughed, and Rusty's baritone chuckle echoed throughout the glade in harmony with itself. Some even mimicked Rusty's startled squawk as the King spun him around in the air, and a handful pretended to spin in the air like a child's top.

The King bellowed: "To the air!"

All of the Rusties launched into the air, flying in a circle around the clearing. And like that, Bormwyn's Rusty, the real Rusty, was lost.

She circled about, disoriented, desperately trying to find her friend, but all that did was make her head spin.

"And down," said the King.

With those words, all of the Rusties landed gently on the ground.

"All you need to do, witchling," said the King, "is pick your friend from our children."

"Without using your magic," added the Queen with a laugh.

"And do it quickly, for once twilight ends, we shall take our leave through the World Door."

"With the lord Guardian, should you fail."

"Or should you not manage to find him by then."

The Queen's eyes shone brightly. "And then the World Door

shall remain unlocked for a year."

Bromwyn felt panic creep into her as her breathing quickened and her heartbeat threatened to become treacherous. How could she dispel an illusion without her magic?

No—she would not panic. She would not give that to the fey, and certainly not so cheaply. Bromwyn forced herself to take a cleansing breath. She didn't need her magic; she needed to outthink the fey.

*When the fey mimic bodies, they do not seem to get it exactly right.*

So she had said to Rusty, after the fey had clothed themselves in likenesses of Jalsa and Brend. The King himself had done only a little better when he had posed as the priest. No matter how close a fey copy was, something about it would be off—the appearance, the attitude, a combination of both. She could do this.

She *would* do this.

"Agreed," whispered Bromwyn, her fists clenching.

The King and Queen both shouted: "Ready, steady, go!"

Bromwyn looked at the hundreds of Rusties that floated a bit off the ground. They were all looking back at her, some quite boldly, and nearly all wore Rusty's half-smile. Just the sight of them was enough to make her feel dizzy.

*They underestimate you,* her grandmother's voice whispered. *They are arrogant.*

"My lord and lady," Bromwyn called out, "I request process of elimination."

A mocking laugh, and then the King said, "Agreed." There was a pause, and then he added, "What of it, my wife? She is just a girl, no matter what her blood."

"Agreed," sniffed the Queen, sounding less than pleased. "A touch or a word from you shall eliminate those you specify. Now begin, or concede. I grow bored."

Bromwyn smiled from the small victory.

*Well then*, she thought. *Let us start with the easy ones.*

Instead of trying to look at all of the Rusties, she focused on them one at a time. Slowly, she began to dismiss those whose costumes were far from the mark: eyes the wrong color, hair too long or too short, the foolish hat too narrow or too small. One by one, she touched those she dismissed, or simply pointed at them and said "No."

And one by one, the false Rusties popped into their previous fey guises of blond hair and blue eyes, their bodies swathed in summer flowers. Once revealed, they flew to the sides of their King and Queen, who stood watching—the King with a wry expression, the Queen with her arms folded across her chest, her face dark.

Bromwyn continued her scrutiny, and she continued dismissing Rusties. Feet too large. Expression too mocking. Teeth too perfectly white and straight. Skin too pale. Skin too dark. Suit too small. Face too old. Nose too big.

And then there were three Rusties left. Only three, from hundreds. And Bromwyn could not tell them apart.

She looked from one to the other to the third, and back again, but they all were the same, down to the pale scar that bisected his left eyebrow, the one that Rusty liked to pretend came from a rogue's sword instead of from him tripping over his own feet and slamming headfirst against the bakery's countertop.

Bromwyn felt another hint of panic, but she pushed it away as she took a deep breath. Then she closed her eyes.

"What is she doing?" asked the King.

"Praying," said the Queen, laughing merrily.

Bromwyn ignored them.

*I know you, Derek Jonasson,* she thought, *the baker's son who would be a thief prince. I know how you smile, how you smirk, how your eyes light up whenever you think of something wicked, which is far too often.*

*I know the sound of your laugh, your musical laugh that does funny things to my stomach and makes my heart want to dance.*

*I know what makes you fret. I know what makes you rage.*

*I know what stirs your heart and what makes you demand impossible things. I know your dreams.*

*I know you, Rusty. And I will not let the fey steal you from me.*

With a nod, she opened her eyes. She peered at the three Rusties, and now she was able to see the slight imperfections: The Rusty in the middle was just a whisper too full in the face, and the Rusty on the left was a hair's width too tall.

Bromwyn motioned to the Rusty on the right. In a clear voice, she announced, "This is the lord Guardian and Key Bearer."

The other two Rusties popped into the blond-haired, blue-eyed guises and blew her kisses before they zoomed off to join their brethren. The true Rusty tumbled to the ground, but he tucked and rolled, then landed with a flourish on his feet and managed somehow to keep his hat atop his head. He grinned at her hugely.

Bromwyn grinned in return. She had done it! Now all they had to do was usher the fey through the World Door, and then lock it behind them.

Two sets of indulgent claps shattered her thoughts.

"Well done," the Queen said lazily, still clapping.

"Yes, yes," said the King, yawning. "Very amusing."

"But it is not really you that we are interested in, witch girl." The Queen smiled. "Now it is time for my lord Guardian's challenge."

Bromwyn blinked. "But ... my lady, I do not understand. We agreed that I was to take the challenge."

The Queen laughed. "And so we did, witch girl. But you never said that you would take it in his place."

"You merely said you wished to take it," said the King, his expression sly.

"And so we readily agreed."

"And now it is his turn." The King smiled a small, cruel smile, one that promise malice. "As agreed, it is a challenge of Sight. And the witchling will not use her magic to aid you."

Bromwyn's mouth went dry, and she found she could not speak. From long ago, she remembered the pixie Nala counseling her, telling her that rules were easy to follow if she was certain of the words—and that was why she must always be careful of what she said.

She hadn't been careful, and now all her turn at the challenge had done was eaten up time.

"Agreed," said Rusty, his voice cracking.

Bromwyn felt invisible bands wrap around her, and suddenly she was hovering in the air. Her instinct was to struggle, but she quashed it. First, it would do her no good, for her power could not begin to measure up to that of the fey lord and lady. Second, it would be undignified. So she clicked her teeth together and held her head up and tried to look bored.

"My children," shouted the Queen. "Look you well."

Bromwyn ignored the leers and mocking cries from the fey horde as she felt their gazes riddle her. She stared at Rusty, tried to tell him with her mind that she believed in him, that she knew he would pass the challenge.

"Now clothe yourselves!"

And then she saw herself—hundreds of copies of herself. Some of the fey were giggling wildly, and roaming their hands over their bodies in a way that made Bromwyn blush fiercely. But she didn't comment on it; let them keep it up, and it would be that much easier for Rusty to dismiss them.

"To the air," the King shouted.

All of the other Bromwyns flew up to cover the air in the clearing. Around the World Door they hovered, some spiraling upside-down so that the long, billowing gown bunched up and showed off long legs.

In her mind, she heard the Queen say: *Now smile.*

Bromwyn's mouth pulled into a soft smile. She struggled against it, but it did no good. Silently fuming, and taking pains to keep her thoughts very, very well hidden, Bromwyn stopped fighting against the fey magic. Her smile stretched wider, and her thoughts grew darker.

To either side of her, her duplicates giggled.

If Bromwyn could have done so, she would have growled in frustration. She sounded nothing like that!

"As the witchling before you," said the King, standing now in front of Bromwyn so that she could see his back, "all you need to do, Key Bearer, is pick the true Bromwyn Darkeyes from our children."

"And the witch girl will not aid you with her magic. This will be all your own skill, my lord Guardian," the Queen purred from somewhere to Bromwyn's left. "Let us see how your silver tongue helps you now."

"Best choose quickly," added the King. "Once twilight ends, we will be gone."

"With you, my lord Guardian, should you fail."

"Or should you not manage to find the witchling before the sun fully rises."

"And should that happen," said the Queen joyfully, "then the World Door shall remain unlocked for a year."

"And we shall return every night," said the King. "And your village will be ours."

"I request the same as Lady Witch," Rusty called out. "Process of elimination!"

Bromwyn would have laughed, had the Queen's magic allowed it. Instead, she was reduced to giggling along with the fey around her.

"Agreed," said the King, sounding bored.

"Agreed," said the Queen, with a sniff of derision.

"Agreed," said Rusty, and Bromwyn could hear the grin in his voice. The thief prince sounded as if he were getting ready for another adventure.

Had it been up to Bromwyn, she would have narrowed her eyes and scolded him, reminding him not to get too cocky. But all she could do was glower at him from inside her mind. Her mouth smiled on.

"Now," Rusty said, "let's get this challenge started. Dawn is coming, and I'm sure that my lord and lady have places to be."

"By all means," said the King with a mocking bow. "Begin."

Thanks to the fey Queen's magic, Bromwyn couldn't move, so she couldn't see where Rusty was. But she heard his voice, loud and confident, as he began to dismiss her copies.

"No. No. Heavens, no. Heh, don't I wish, but no. No. No. Argh, absolutely not. No. Nope. Alas, no." And so on. A number of times, Rusty stopped in front of Bromwyn, and each time, her heart would skip. He would stare deeply into her eyes, then appraise her as if she were a prized horse. She wanted to kiss him and slap him. Surely, he had to know her from the fey.

And surely, he didn't have to ogle her!

So it went, and the sky slowly lightened. With every rejection of her duplicates, Bromwyn felt more confident, and when an abundance of her copies had been ousted, she wanted to cheer until she was hoarse.

Finally, only one copy and Bromwyn herself were left.

Her duplicate floated directly across from her, and even to

Bromwyn it seemed as if she were looking into a mirror. Rusty was staring at the copy intently, then back at Bromwyn herself. He took off his hat and raked his hair with his fingers. Then he replaced the hat, the wide brim shadowing his face—but not before Bromwyn saw the sheen of panic in his eyes.

He didn't know.

*Me,* she shouted with her mind. *Me, Rusty, here! You must know me!* She continued to smile blandly, though she wanted to scream with all of her heart.

Rusty took a deep breath and pointed to the other girl, and Bromwyn felt a wave of pure relief wash over her. Now he would dismiss her final copy, and they will have bested the fey at their own game.

But then Rusty said, "This one. This is Lady Witch."

*No.*

Bromwyn couldn't move, couldn't scream, couldn't do anything but watch the other Bromwyn open her arms to Rusty, who leaned in to embrace her. And then her fey duplicate kissed him on his brow.

*No!*

Bromwyn barely felt the Queen's spell unravel before she was falling. With a thump, she crashed heavily on the ground. Biting her lip to keep from screaming, she scrambled to her feet and ran over to Rusty.

He was staring at nothing. A dazed smile had frozen upon his face.

When Bromwyn grabbed him out of her duplicate's arms, he

didn't respond. She shook him, even slapped his cheek, but all he did was smile, mesmerized.

He was marked, lost forever in the thrall of fey magic.

*Please,* Bromwyn thought desperately, *please no!*

The Queen laughed, a sound like leaves rustling in the wind. "It would seem, witch girl, that you lose."

# TO BREAK A CURSE

"No," Bromwyn whispered.

Her denial was lost amidst the cheering of the fey. They screamed their joy, stamping their feet and whooping laughter, somersaulting through the air and spiraling through the clearing. Drums beat wildly as the fey danced their victory, chattering and jibing, riding the wind and stretching their limbs long as if to embrace the coming sun.

Rusty was pulled away from her and passed around like a toy.

Bromwyn sank to her knees, her hands by her mouth, her head shaking "no" and "no" and "no."

The King and Queen soared through the air, filling the glade with the scent of honeysuckle in the rain. Bromwyn watched them, too stunned to look away. As the King danced with her, the Queen's emerald hair fanned out in a lush wave, sparkling with diamond chips. The blue silk of his shirt and trousers flowed like water, and the flowers of her gown and his cloak rippled as they moved. They laughed, and Bromwyn's world fell apart.

She had failed—failed to protect Rusty, failed to pass her test. Failed to protect Loren. The fey would return every night, and they would steal away the village's children, or lure them with false promises or seduce them with petty prizes. The children would be theirs, as would the adults, for even iron could keep the fey at a distance for only so long before they would find some way around it.

And then they would feast.

The drums beat; the laughter swelled. Bromwyn covered her ears, squeezed her eyes shut. But it was too late to deaden her senses. The smells, the sounds, the sights were enchanting— everything shimmered with fey magic, beckoning to her to join them in their dance, to laugh with them in their celebration. To cheer with them in their victory.

To be with them, to do anything they asked, to live only to hear them laugh.

To love them with all of her heart.

The only thing that stopped her from throwing herself into the midst of the dance was seeing Rusty, stumbling from fey to fey, being pushed round and round in a circle as he smiled on, sightless.

*Oh, Rusty.* Bromwyn's heart broke as she watched him stagger-dance like a puppet. *Forgive me.*

"My children!"

Bromwyn tore her gaze from Rusty to see the King hovering in front of the World Door, his arms out.

"The sky bleeds gold, and the magic of twilight gives way to the harsh dawn. Day fast approaches. And so, shed your skins and prepare for travel. Through the World Door, my children. But worry not," he added, gloating. "For we will return this evening, and the next, and the next after that!"

The fey shrieked their joy, and then they folded in on themselves and shrank until they were points of golden light no larger than bumblebees. They buzzed their laughter, and they shimmered and sparkled in the light of all colors that was the World Door. As a swarm, they zoomed around the clearing one last time before they surged through the gap between realities and were gone.

The line of stars over the stones of the Hill seemed to wink, and the Door sighed. Like a dreamer slowly waking, the World Door yawned. In a matter of minutes, it would be closed.

Closed, but not locked.

Along with the Door, the clearing held only the Queen and King, and a spellbound Rusty. And Bromwyn, of course, beaten and left with nothing but to await her grandmother's judgment before her magic was shorn from her.

Even now, she could hear her grandmother's voice, warning her that the fey were arrogant.

And they were; it was their arrogance that caused them to allow Bromwyn to slightly alter the rules of the challenge to accommodate process of elimination, even after the allotted time had passed.

But her grandmother had told her something else about the fey.

She remembered the note that had waited for her in Niove's kitchen, remembered the advice her grandmother had written in her spidery script: *Keep in mind what the fey value most.*

What did the arrogant truly want? What could she offer them?

She remembered King's voice, from years gone:

*I could give you your wish, Bromwyn Darkeyes. Come with me and my lady Queen. Join us as we go through the World Door at dawn to return to our land. There you will have no rules. There you may run and play and dance among the stars. What say you?*

The King wanted *her*, Bromwyn realized with a start. He had, when she was a child. And last night, even in the throes of his taunting, she had seen in his eyes that he had wanted Bromwyn to join him. She had felt it in her heart.

*You would have had a place in my Court as a daughter,* he had told her. *Was it so much to ask that you love me with all of your heart, young Darkeyes?*

"Please," she begged the King now, him and Queen both, "please, my lord, my lady, please. Take me instead."

There was a pause, through which Bromwyn heard her own ragged breathing. And then the Queen barked out a laugh.

"And why ever would we do that, witch girl? Our hunger is for humans." The Queen smiled coyly. "You hold no special appeal. Fey magic courses through your veins."

Her words thundered in Bromwyn's ears, and she remembered how she had overcome the fire in Master Tiller's fields, how the heat had stayed with her when she had cast a spell of Sight upon her hand and threatened to burn the fey.

She thought of how she had never known her father, only that he had died soon after he and her mother had wed.

She remembered the wretched things the King and Queen had insinuated about her mother, and for a moment, a horrible moment that seemed to eat the entire world, she wondered who her father truly had been.

*They lie,* she told herself fiercely. *The fey lie. They trick and they trade, they bend truth and stretch it until it breaks. Do not listen to them.*

The King put out his hand, and his lady wife fell silent. He looked at Bromwyn, his gaze cutting, his smile cruel.

"I told you, did I not? I told you I would never again offer you a place in our land. Did you not believe me?"

No, this wasn't right! He was supposed to tell her that yes, he wanted her to join them! She tried to catch her breath, but it wisped away from her, like smoke drifting on the wind.

"My lord," Bromwyn stammered, "I offer to take the Guardian's place. As a page, as a slave, as however you and your lady Queen would have me."

The King chuckled softly.

"Whatever you wanted," Bromwyn said, desperation making her voice stronger, "I would do."

His voice low, the King asked her, "And if I were to agree, would you love me with all of your heart, young Darkeyes, as do all of my fey children?"

The Queen snorted.

"Yes," Bromwyn whispered, knowing it was a lie, but she would have told him anything to save Rusty. Yes, she would agree to that, and more. Yes, a thousand times yes.

For Rusty, she would agree to sign away her soul.

The King's laugh hit her like a slap. "A pity, then, that I must refuse." His voice dripped with scorn. "Unlike some, I do not go back on my word."

Bromwyn bit her lip to keep from sobbing, but she couldn't stop her tears. She had lost. And now Rusty and the village of Loren would pay the price. And pay. And pay, until they were bled dry.

"Such pain," the Queen chortled. "Only the young can sound so heartbroken and yet so outraged. How it hurts her to swallow her pride!"

"Look, I see tears on those cold cheeks!" The King laughed heartily. "She cries for this boy."

"She does," said the Queen. "See how her tears shine like jewels!"

The King's laughter faded, leaving only the hint of an echo in the wind. "Tell me, witchling," he said, his words surrounded by that ghost of amusement. "What is your claim on this one boy? Why does one little life matter to you so very much?"

"He is my friend," Bromwyn said, her voice cracking on the last word.

"Her *friend*," the Queen scoffed.

Bromwyn could no longer meet the King's bemused gaze, so she looked at her hands. "Yes, my friend. And more than that," she admitted softly. "So much more. I love him."

She loved him.

She felt it deep in her heart, knew it in her soul: She loved him. Derek Jonasson, the baker's son; Rusty, the thief prince. Whatever name he went by, however he saw himself, she loved him. She wanted to be by his side, whether on mad adventures around the world or on the most tedious of errands for their mothers. She wanted to shout her joy to the skies and declare herself before all of Nature, and by Fire and Air, she didn't care whether others agreed. She loved Rusty, and she would do anything for him.

She *loved* him.

Her heart seemed to swell, and her mouth opened so that she could cry out, could gasp, could say something, say *anything*, for there was a bubble in her chest, a feeling of intense pressure, and she was certain that she was about to die.

And then she felt it: a gentle pop, a tiny *pfft* that was the release of magic back into the fabric of Nature itself. Her hair and gown rippled in a sudden breeze, and the very air around her glowed as she sat there, beneath the Hill, and even the stars of the World Door paled in comparison. A shiver ran through her, and she breathed in—truly breathed, like she hadn't for years. Her skin thrummed with power as her grandmother's curse unraveled, and then, finally, she was free.

"I love him," she said again, her voice no longer a whisper.

She rose gracefully, feeling so very alive, thrilling from the power of life dancing through her, dancing in her, life as strong as magic itself, connecting her to Nature and to all living things. Bromwyn Elmindrea Lucinda Moon, called Darkeyes, companion to the Guardian of the World Door and next in line to be the Wise One of Loren, stared into the mocking eyes of the fey King, and she smiled.

"I love him," she said a third time. "That is my claim."

# THE PRICE OF A SOUL

"Love." The Queen smirked, and Bromwyn thought it an ugly thing on such an enchanting face. "We know of love, witch girl."

"Why else would we steal human children?" asked the King.

"Truly, my lord," said Bromwyn, lifting her chin, "I do not know, other than to cause unceasing pain to their parents."

The King snorted. "We are not so crass as that. We steal them so that they can become our children."

"We love human children as if they were our own," said the Queen, taking her husband's hand.

"And in our land, they become our own."

"And so the fey survive."

"And thrive."

"Forever and always," the Queen said, smiling at her husband, who kissed her hand as he gazed lovingly upon her.

Bromwyn wondered whether it was the King or the Queen who could not have children in the traditional sense, but she knew better than to ask such a delicate question. So instead she said, "You say you know of love. Well and good. But do you respect my claim?"

The King gave his wife's hand a final kiss before releasing it. "I have little doubt that you love him," he said, motioning to Rusty. "But that does not change the fact that the Key Bearer lost our challenge."

"And as per the rules that both parties agreed to," said the Queen, "that means he is ours."

Bromwyn wanted to scream, wanted to cast her magic wide and grab Fire and roast them alive. But no—she would not cast out of anger or fear. She had to keep her wits about her.

"Do not fret," said the Queen, smiling lushly. "He will make a lovely addition to my Court."

Fire and Air, Bromwyn had not broken her grandmother's curse only to have the boy she loved taken from her! But how could she fight the King and Queen? Their magic was far stronger than hers. She could not defeat them in terms of sheer power.

Then how?

"And who knows?" the King said, his grin a thing of horrors. "Perhaps in a few years, we will allow him to return to his homeland, just to pay you a very special visit."

Her voice tight, Bromwyn replied, "I have not the words to convey my lord's kindness."

*You cannot prepare for a fey challenge,* her grandmother had told her.

*All you can do is try to outthink them.*

But how could she outthink the fey, who were such sticklers for rules and agreements?

"Come, my page." The Queen held out her hand, and Rusty took it, smiling and unaware. With a laugh, the Queen drew him close, and she petted his shoulder. "It will be quite fun to housebreak you."

The world threatened to tunnel down to red, and Bromwyn's head throbbed with the effort of schooling her face to impassivity. She refused to give the fey the satisfaction of seeing her impotent fury. Her fingers itched to cast, and for a fleeting moment, she thought she could cast from Sight—blind them, grab Rusty, and run. But no, that was pure foolishness; her magic was worse than useless when compared to the power of the fey King and Queen. Bromwyn's hands trembled from the need to do something. Helpless, she shoved them into the pockets of her dress.

Her fingers brushed against the iron key.

"We shall see you tonight, witch girl," the Queen said happily, turning to face the World Door. "But perhaps you should consider finding a new place to call your home. Starting tonight, you will find your charming village to be undergoing the first of many changes."

Bromwyn cried out, "Wait!"

"What now?" the King said impatiently. "You have nothing that we want, and our time here is done. For today, at least."

"But I do," said Bromwyn, her thoughts whirling. "I have something that you want very much."

219

The King arched a brow, and the Queen paused, with Rusty in tow.

"Well?" the Queen demanded. "What is it?"

*Remember what the fey value most.*

"I offer a trade," Bromwyn declared. "A gift, in exchange for the lord Guardian here and now. Unmarked, unharmed, soul intact. What say you?"

"What sort of gift could it possibly be?" the Queen scoffed. "You have nothing to offer."

"In that, my lady, you are incorrect." Bromwyn smiled, and it felt sweet on her face. "I have something in my possession that is more than equal to the value of one human's soul. In fact," she added slowly, "it is so much greater that I would be a fool to accept only the lord Guardian, safe and sound."

"She is mad," the Queen said. "Driven to the point of insanity over losing her love and earning her grandmother's ire. Oh," she purred, "the Whitehair will destroy you, witch girl. Come, my husband. Let us go."

"My wife, hold." The King gazed at Bromwyn as if trying to seek out the truth behind her smile. "I admit, I am most curious. I would know what she believes to be of equal value to a human soul."

"Of *greater* value, my lord." Bromwyn inclined her head. "Even an unworldly girl such as myself recognizes the importance of such a prize."

"How much greater?" asked the King, and Bromwyn heard the hunger in his voice.

Her fingers wrapped around the Key. "Significantly."

"She lies," the Queen said impatiently. "Do you not see that? The sun rises. We must go."

The King stared long and hard at Bromwyn before he finally spoke. "I propose this: Should you be correct, witchling, I will not only relinquish our claim to the boy but also to your land. We would allow you to lock the World Door, and we would not return for a year's time. But," he said, "if you are wrong, and your gift is of lesser value, then the Door remains unlocked for the year, the boy remains with us, and your life will be mine. No feeble claim of protection by your village's laws would save you, just as your friend was not saved. If you are wrong, you will lose everything."

There was a pause, filled only by the Allenswood slowly waking in the coming dawn.

"Unlike my lady wife, I myself have little use for pages. But I do so enjoy blood that is spiced with magic." The King stared at Bromwyn, his gaze as biting as winter frost. "What say you, witchling? Do you still boast to hold something worth all of that?"

Her heart thumping madly, her breath ragged, Bromwyn said, "I do."

"Then are we agreed?"

"Yes, my lord. Agreed."

He smiled triumphantly, and once again Bromwyn smelled springtime rain. But instead of a heady, overwhelming scent, she found it merely pleasant, like a favorite memory.

The King asked, "What do you have in your possession that you insist is of greater value than this boy's soul?"

With a small smile of her own, Bromwyn pulled out the Key from her pocket. "My gift to you is the Key to the World Door."

There was silence in the glade as the stars twinkled over the stones of the Hill and the Door edged that much closer to shutting.

Bromwyn's heartbeat galloped, and her head felt oddly light. Giddy, she watched the King's face slowly darken, and the whiff of spring rain transformed into the stink of a sudden storm. Bromwyn felt as if she were drowning—or, perhaps, that she was the one holding the King's head beneath the water.

"You are not the Key Bearer," he said coldly. "It is not yours to give."

Bromwyn smiled even more. "It came into my possession just before we met you for the challenge, my lord. It was given to me freely by the lord Guardian."

"She tells the truth," the Queen spat. "I see it in her heart, as clearly as the diluted magic that rushes through her body. The boy gave her the Key."

"And it is my offering to you, most noble of the fair folk. Is it not at least equal to the life of one human boy?" Bromwyn pressed on, encouraged by the looks of anger that passed between the fey sovereigns. "What is one boy's soul, compared with the force that opens pathways of reality?"

"A most impressive gift," the King said, voice flat.

"Quite," the Queen agreed, murder shining in her eyes.

"But the Key is made of iron," said the King.

"We cannot touch it."

"Nor can we wield it with our magic."

"It is completely useless to us."

"A most vexing gift," the King said, nostrils flaring.

Bromwyn dipped her head in the smallest of bows, acknowledging their points. "That is unfortunate, my lord, my lady. Be that as it may, is the Key of equal or greater value than one boy's soul?"

The Queen hissed, "Impertinent girl!"

"She is," the King said quietly. "Oh, indeed, she is. Well played, witchling."

"Leave open the World Door," snarled the Queen, "and we will release our claim on the boy!"

"No, my lady." Bromwyn stood tall, felt the power of that simple word resonate through the clearing. "I have offered you a trade that is worth far more than the lord Guardian's soul. I have met your demands. And now you will meet mine. Unless," she added, "you wish to renege."

The word hung in the air, festering like disease.

"You *dare*," the Queen spat. "You think we would ever relinquish our power over the fate of one human boy?"

Bromwyn couldn't help but grin. "Many years ago, it was a pixie who had taught me a most important rule. And that rule was this: Magic always has rules. My lady, I thank you for sharing freely with me the rule of your own magic."

The Queen snarled her fury.

"So," the King said, laughing softly. "Your little game has come back to haunt you, my lady wife. Your ploy to trick the witchling out of the safety of the Whitehair's home worked too well. Instead of us taking her humanity, you gave her knowledge."

"I gave her no such thing!" the Queen thundered.

"You were careless, and she was clever."

Bromwyn's eyes widened as she understood the meaning behind their words: That long ago Midsummer when she had escaped her grandmother's cottage, it hadn't been a simple pixie who had helped her in want of a playmate.

It had been the fey Queen in disguise, seeking to do mischief upon Niove Whitehair's grandchild.

Bromwyn curtsied to hide her smile. "Your generosity is boundless, my lady," she said, "even as your beauty is legendary."

"As is my anger." The Queen's grin was a monstrous thing of fangs, and Bromwyn felt the air charge with magic. "I will pull the skin from your body and use it for my bed gown! I will break all of your bones to suck out the marrow within! I will bathe in your blood!"

Bromwyn would have been terrified if she hadn't seen the King's face. She had won; it was all but written on his features. She had beaten them at their own game. And she had learned something nearly as valuable as the Key itself: If the fey went back on their word, they lost their power.

So instead of casting her magic in anger or flinging out hasty words to see if they scored, Bromwyn smiled and waited.

The Key was heavy in her palm.

"My lady wife," the King murmured, "that is quite enough."

Bromwyn met the Queen's terrible gaze, and for a moment she saw the monster beneath the woman's guise. It rippled beneath her skin like a sea serpent undulating beneath the waves, and when she spoke, it became a kraken's growl. "She is her grandmother's kin, no doubt!"

"And her mother's daughter," the King said with an ugly smile. "We accept your gift of the Key, Bromwyn Darkeyes. As agreed, we release our claim on this boy and on this land. For the next year, at least. My lady wife, let the boy go."

The Queen glowered at Bromwyn, but she said, "As my lord husband requests."

There was a flash of magic, and a white light flared over Rusty's head. Then he crashed to the ground, a puppet with its strings cut.

Bromwyn didn't dare go to his side; she was too busy staring down the raging Queen.

"As we cannot touch your gift," said the King, "we must ask that you hold it for us in good faith, and that you present the Key to us next Midsummer."

Bromwyn swallowed thickly, but her voice was steady when she replied, "I most graciously accept your charge as Key Bearer."

"Thank you, my lady Guardian." The King's smile was mocking, but it lacked its earlier cruel edge. His eyes, however, held little mirth; instead, they were hooded and cunning.

Oh, Bromwyn was in so much trouble. Thankfully, she had a full year to figure out how to best work her way out of it.

"By your leave," the Queen snarled. Without waiting for a reply, she spun on her heel and leapt through the World Door.

"You have proven to be quite entertaining, witchling." The King smiled slyly. "The same as your mother before you, albeit for different reasons."

Bromwyn felt her anger stir, but she allowed it to bubble without letting it run over. She had learned that much, at least. She replied, "My grandmother had hoped that I would provide you with some alternative entertainment this year, my lord. The last thing she wants is for you and your lady wife to be bored."

"Indeed," he said, snorting. "She is a clever one, for her kind."

"She has been called that."

"Among other things, I imagine." The King stared at Bromwyn, his eyes alight with magic and mischief and rage. "Know that we shall issue a different challenge next Midsummer, witchling, one that will not be nearly so lenient."

Bromwyn's heart froze in her chest, but she said, "I thank my lord for fair warning."

"All of the time in the world will not help you." The King bowed low. "Build your strength. Cast your spells. Pray to your gods. It matters not. Nothing shall save you." He stood tall, a dangerous smile on his face. "Next Midsummer, your life will belong to me. This promises Aeric, King of the fey and lord of all of the timeless lands."

Bromwyn bit back a gasp. His name. He had just given her his name.

His smile stretched to inhuman proportions. "Until that time, Bromwyn Darkeyes, farewell." With those words, he stepped through the World Door and vanished.

"Well now," Rusty said weakly from the ground. "They certainly do know how to make an exit."

# THE WORLD DOOR CLOSES

Bromwyn rushed over to where Rusty lay, nearly tripping over the hem of her gown in her haste. His hat had flown off, and he was sprawled in the grass, all beanpole length and a tangle of limbs, his red hair seeming to catch fire in the dawn. His face was blanched, and shock danced in his eyes.

She paused before him, terrified that something inside of him had broken, whether in spirit or mind or body.

"Rusty—" Her voice cracked, and she had to fight back a sob. "Are you well?"

He lifted his head up to look at her, grinned like a madman, and then dropped his head back down.

"Ouch," he said. "I feel all sorts of strange."

"You look even stranger." Stumbling to her knees before him, she grabbed him by his jacket lapels and hefted him up until he was in a sitting position, and then she crushed him to her chest in an embrace that would have impressed mother bears. She hugged him tightly, never wanting to let him go.

And when he managed to wrap his arms around her in return, so much the better.

Bromwyn laughed, feeling lighter than air. He was all right! They had survived the encounter with the fey, and the World Door would soon be closed and locked, and then they were free!

For a year, anyway.

She bit her lip as the wonderful floating feeling was replaced with a steel ball in her gut. No, an iron ball.

And even without the Key, she and Rusty were still bound to their obligations in Loren: his to the bakery and his parents, hers to Brend and her magic.

Had she really thought they were free?

*Well, never mind all of that,* she decided, hugging Rusty all the harder, until he complained about his ribs creaking. Later, there would be time to fret over how they were still trapped by their responsibilities. Later, they could rage against the world, or even plot to steal away in the cover of night and escape to some remote land, where they would be left alone to do whatever they wished, whenever they wished.

Silly thoughts, she knew, but she figured that she was allowed a little silliness. For a little while longer, they could bask in simply being alive.

"Winnie?" Rusty's voice was soft, and loving, and altogether perfect. "Are you laughing? Or crying?"

"Laughing, of course," she said, sniffling hard. "Witches never cry."

"And they live in candy houses. I've read the stories." He wheezed out a chuckle. "Damn me, I hurt. What happened?"

"You lost the challenge, but I tricked them into giving you back to me, and going away for the year." She frowned, and then she clouted the back of his head.

"Hey!" He pulled away from her, rubbing the sore spot. "What was that for?"

"For not picking correctly." She crossed her arms. "How could you possibly think that fey girl was me?"

"What? Are you serious?"

"Of course I am serious! She looked nothing like me!"

He gaped at her.

"And do not think I did not hear you as you dismissed the others. I distinctly recall you saying something about wishing one of them actually was me." She glared at him. "Why? Did she have more ... wenchly assets?"

The corners of Rusty's mouth flitted up in a smile, and his right cheek dimpled. He said, "'Wenchly'?"

"Was she prettier? What was better about her than me?"

Rusty chuckled softly, and he reached out to stroke Bromwyn's cheek. Try as she might to be indignant, she found herself leaning into the touch.

"Winnie," he said, smiling warmly, "there's no comparison.

Nothing could be better than you."

She blinked away sudden tears. "So why did you say such a thing?"

"Well, it was either try to joke, or vomit out of sheer nerves. And that would have gotten all over my boots."

Bromwyn giggled, and then she stared deeply into his eyes. Just looking into them made it seem like anything was possible.

"I was so worried for you," she said, her voice full. "Rusty, if you had gone with them, I would have died."

"Your granny does have a temper, doesn't she?"

She clouted the back of his head again. "No, you foolish boy. I would have died of heartbreak."

"And I'll die from your backhand," he said, grinning hugely. "Help me up, if you please."

As she pulled him to his feet, twilight gave way to sunrise. The last breaths of gray evaporated into gold-tinted daylight. Over the flat stones, the stars shimmered, dazzling Bromwyn as they sparkled in all colors and none, pulsing with the magic that was the reality between all worlds. And then the clearing shook with a thunderous *BOOM!*

Bromwyn couldn't help but smile when Rusty wrapped his arms around her as if to shield her from the sound. He was such a *boy*.

And if she snuggled into his arms as the booming echoed around them, well, what of it?

After all was silent, Bromwyn gently pulled away and turned to face the World Door—or, more accurately, where the Door had been. Closed once again, all that was left were the large stones forming a circle on the Hill, their flat surfaces catching the rays of the morning sun, suggesting the faintest hint of starlight twinkling.

Holding the Key by its oval base, Bromwyn approached the stones. Slowly, walking widdershins, she bent down and tapped the Key against each stone, dead center, exactly once. After each tap, the stone's light winked out, and at the end, Bromwyn was standing outside a ring of ordinary flat stones that once a year became an extraordinary gateway.

"That's it?" Rusty called out. "It's locked now?"

"Yes." With one last look at the Hill, Bromwyn walked back to Rusty, who was now standing at the far end of the glade. His foppish hat was once again perched atop his head, the brim down at a rakish angle. Bromwyn thought he looked wonderful. She said, "Grandmother used to complain about locking the Door."

"Why? Did she hate to see the fairies leave?"

"The bending was murder on her back."

Rusty grinned. "No wonder she's always in such a foul mood."

"No," Bromwyn said, slipping the Key into her pocket, "that is just her temperament."

"You shouldn't keep that in your pocket. It could fall out."

"Or get stolen," she said dryly.

"Oh, no worries about that. If there's one person's pockets I avoid, it's yours."

"I always suspected that you were smart." A huge yawn cracked her jaw.

"Don't do that," Rusty scolded, yawning in return. "Damn me, I could sleep for a week."

She smiled tiredly. "Saving the village is exhausting work."

"You're right. Let's not do it again." Rusty offered his hand to her. "Come on, let's head back. Maybe there's time for a nap before everything returns to normal."

*Normal.* The word didn't seem a good fit for her life any longer. She had so many questions that flitted in her mind, half-formed and ticklish like will o' the wisps. The King and Queen had said unsettling things, disturbing things that made Bromwyn's skin turn cold just thinking about them.

*Fey magic courses through your veins.*

The fey lied, but they also told the truth. The problem was determining which was which.

And then there was the small matter of being in love with a boy who was decidedly not the man to whom she was promised to marry in a few months' time.

The only saving grace was that she was too tired to think properly, let alone fret. At the moment, the only concern she had was getting home before she fell asleep standing up.

So she entwined her fingers around Rusty's, and the two of them slowly made their way back to the village.

# PART 5: FIVE HOURS LATER

# ENDINGS

# TO FAIL A TEST

Bromwyn slept fitfully. Dreams plagued her, causing her to twitch and mutter, and when she awoke a bare few hours after she had returned home, she felt as if she'd been run down by one of Master Tiller's oxen. Her head throbbed mercilessly, and it was much too heavy for her neck. With a groan, she swung her legs off of her straw-filled mattress, fighting the blankets that had tangled around her limbs. When she pulled herself to her feet, the room began to sway.

If there was no rest for the wicked, as she'd heard it said, then those of good intent fared little better.

She didn't understand why she felt as if she were still wrestling with her sheets until she looked down, and nearly lost her balance from the effort. Fire and Air, her head really *was* too heavy! As she steadied herself, she realized that she was still wearing her mother's blue dress, and she vaguely recalled being too exhausted to strip out of it. The garment was rumpled, possibly even ruined, and the girdle that had done such interesting (and rather embarrassing) things to her bosom had loosened and now was slung around her hips. When she raised her hand to brush away a snarl of hair, it felt as if a wet cat had taken up residence atop her head, and she moaned as she recalled all of the pins and combs and nameless things that had been glued into her thick tresses.

At least she'd had enough sense to kick off her shoes before she'd fallen into her bed.

Eyes stinging, head pounding, she pushed aside the curtain that separated her room from the main part of the dwelling. Her mother had not yet set up shop for the day—no fine cloth covered the large table in the center of the floor, and no candles had yet been lit. Indeed, Jessamin's cards were nowhere in sight.

Bromwyn could not recall the last time her mother did not have the shop that was their home ready for a customer's visit.

Jessamin stood by the fire pit in the corner, filling a teapot with water from the cauldron. She glanced over at Bromwyn as the curtain settled back into place, and she smiled fondly at her daughter.

"Good morning!" she said brightly. "Yes, it is still morning, albeit barely. Today I would have let you sleep until tonight. You deserve to sleep in, after your activities overnight. Why are you up so soon? You have barely been abed for four hours!"

Bromwyn opened her mouth to reply, but her mother continued:

"Poor girl. Last night's finery is this morning's misery. Let me help you get untangled. Just as well, for the tea needs time to steep. There are three things that simply cannot be rushed: childbirth, cooking, and steeping tea."

Bromwyn could barely keep up with her mother's words. She blinked sleepily and said, "What—?"

But Jessamin had already set the teapot onto the table and hurried over to her daughter, clucking over the state of her dress. "The girdle may be saved, but the gown is fit only for burning. The shoes—please tell me you brought back the shoes? Yes? Good— clearly, the shoes left their marks on your feet, if there are indeed feet somewhere beneath all the dirt. By Nature's grace, Daughter, how do you get yourself so filthy? Is it some innate talent of yours, or do you practice at it? And your hair—well. Let us start with that, shall we?"

It took the better part of an hour for her mother to loosen the thick tresses of hair from their prison. Then she helped her daughter free herself from her clothing and filled the large tub for her to bathe, being sure to include herbs to soften the skin and perfume the air. When Bromwyn protested that she would simply get dirty again when she helped the villagers clean up after the destructive Midsummer night, Jessamin threatened to scrub her like a baby.

So Bromwyn bathed. And she pondered.

When the water cooled, she stepped out of the tub and dried herself, first her body, which was quick, and then her hair, which was not. Soon she was dressed and once again in the large room.

Her mother offered her a cup of tea, which she gratefully accepted. It tasted like wildflowers and sugar, and for a moment, she remembered the overwhelming scent of honeysuckle after a spring rain.

*Do you think,* the Queen had asked idly, *that she will follow in her mother's footsteps?*

Bromwyn sipped her tea and looked at her mother, who sat across from her. Fine lines had been etched upon Jessamin's brow, and deeper ones crinkled at the corners of her eyes. Her black hair, pulled into its numerous braids that didn't quite reach her shoulders, was peppered with white.

It had begun to turn two years ago, right after Bromwyn had used her magic in anger.

Shadows bruised the skin beneath Jessamin's eyes, and though she was smiling, Bromwyn saw that her smile was just a pantomime of happiness. Beneath it, her pain was all too clear. The years without her magic and her love had left their mark upon her.

"I am afraid I have lost your books," Bromwyn said sheepishly. "As everything happened last night, I accidentally left them in the Allenswood. By dawn, they were gone. I am truly sorry."

Jessamin waved off the apology. "Pish-tosh. I do not care to think of the fey, so their absence does me a favor. So, you have passed your test." She smiled proudly, though there was a touch of sadness at the corners. "I knew you would pass. You are a better witch than I ever was."

Embarrassed, Bromwyn murmured, "Thank you."

"Well." Jessamin clapped her hands once. "You must speak

with your grandmother as soon as your tea is finished. She will tell you what is to happen next with your studies."

"But the village needs to be cleaned up after what happened overnight."

"That has been under way for hours. Let the others do what they can to help the village return to normal. You have already played your part." She reached over and gently brushed aside an errant lock of hair from Bromwyn's forehead. "Besides, your grandmother is expecting you."

Bromwyn nodded and sipped her tea, and she regretted what she needed to do next.

Life could be cruel, her mother had said yesterday, and fate could be crueler still. But truth, Bromwyn decided, could be the cruelest of all.

It was time for her to be cruel.

She set her cup upon the table. "The King and Queen spoke of you," she said slowly. "They said terrible things. I must ask you, Mother, if they were true things."

Something dark passed over Jessamin's face. "Have you learned nothing from your grandmother? The fey lie. That is what they do: They lie and trick and steal."

"They said I had fey blood in my veins."

Her mother hissed a startled breath, and then she closed her eyes.

"Please," Bromwyn implored. "Do not leave me with their vague accusations. Tell me what they meant."

Jessamin bowed her head so that her short braids hid her face.

When she finally spoke, she didn't look at her daughter.

"It started with a boy," she said, her voice thick. "A beautiful boy from Mooreston. He was the weaver's apprentice there. I saw him time and again, when your grandmother and I would meet with Old Gilla and her apprentice to parley and share castings."

In all of Bromwyn's years as an apprentice, she had never been invited to travel with Niove to meet other witches. She pretended that her mother's words did not sting.

"I was a poor student," Jessamin admitted, "and tended to steal away the first chance I could. Oh, how that vexed your grandmother. She had many words for me after I would do such a thing. And yet, she always brought me to Mooreston, and I would always sneak away to the brook and dip my feet into the cold water. The fish would come close and nibble like quick kisses upon my toes. That is where he found me one afternoon. Oren."

Bromwyn stirred. That was her father's name.

"We talked. We laughed. He, too, enjoyed the feeling of the fish tickling his toes, and we sat with our bare feet splashing in the brook. When I returned home, my thoughts were full of the weaver's apprentice." Her mother paused. "Have you ever worked a casting from the Way of the Heart, Daughter?"

"No."

"To cast, you must lose yourself to the magic of Nature and trust it to keep you safe as you work with it; if you show any restraint, the spell will unravel. The Way of the Heart makes you vulnerable, but if you trust in it completely, it also makes you infallible. What you give, you receive." Jessamin sighed. "It is very much like being in love."

Bromwyn nodded her understanding.

"Being with Oren was like casting from the Heart. He made me lose myself and find myself all at once. He made me feel truly alive. A year and a day after we first met, we pledged our love beneath the moon. It was his name, you see, Oren Moon, and it was both something of a joke to him and yet completely serious: He made all vows in moonlight."

"Rather like a witch," Bromwyn said.

"Yes." Jessamin paused again, and a shadow passed over her face. "Two months after that, he disappeared. The villagers in Mooreston thought he must have drowned, and the fish that he had so enjoyed must have enjoyed themselves in turn upon his flesh. But I knew otherwise. I had begged your grandmother to return him from the dead, and she told me that she could not return what she did not have. He was still alive. Missing, but alive."

"Mother," Bromwyn said quietly, "I am sorry."

Jessamin quickly wiped her eyes. "With Oren gone," she said, "there was nothing left for me but my magic. And so I finally became the apprentice your grandmother had always wanted. I was dutiful. Studious. The following summer was the test of my Way. Your grandmother gave me the Key to the World Door and good advice that I did not believe I needed. And so I found myself the Guardian, with the King and Queen of the fey dancing overhead. I presented them with the rules of decorum, and they gave me their condition in return: I was not to use my magic during their visit. I readily agreed. The terms were set, and we sipped sweet wine, and I watched the fey celebrate Midsummer in the Allenswood."

Bromwyn waited.

"I was careless," said her mother. "The fey saw my darkest heart, and one of them, a river hag, approached me. She knew where my lost love was, she said to me. He had fallen into a waygate at the water's edge."

Bromwyn had read of such gates, pockets of magic that swallowed the unwary traveler and spat them out somewhere within the fey lands—with no way to return.

"The hag promised to fetch him for me and return him through the World Door that very evening if I would do one thing for her: Give her a love potion. I agreed."

"You bargained with the fey?" Bromwyn asked, shocked.

"I would have done anything to see Oren once more," Jessamin insisted. "Yes, I bargained with the river hag. I gave her a potion that would seduce even creatures with the hardest of hearts, and she gave me Oren. But the hag had been the Queen in disguise, and she had tricked me into breaking the compact made earlier that evening."

Bromwyn thought of a pixie at the window, and she grimaced. The Queen did so enjoy her disguises.

"The King challenged me for the right to return every night for a year, to walk freely in the land with no restrictions." Jessamin sighed. "It was your grandmother's quick thinking that saved the village. She spoke quietly with the Queen while the King gloated in front of me, and then your grandmother flattered him with a suggestion of a toast to his victory. But it was the Queen, influenced by your grandmother's words, who put the love potion into the King's cup."

"Were they not already husband and wife?" Bromwyn asked. "Why did she need to enchant the King to win his love?"

Her mother let out a humorless laugh. "Do I need to tell you of arranged marriages and loveless lives, Daughter?"

Bromwyn blushed and bit her lip.

"The King, newly smitten, rescinded his challenge in his rush to return with his lady Queen to their land and do the things that husbands and wives do when they are in love. The World Door closed with the fey tucked away on their side, and your grandmother locked the way behind them." Jessamin took a deep breath. "And in the circle of stones on the great Hill in the Allenswood, your grandmother cut my hair. I had failed my test as Guardian, and I lost my magic."

Bromwyn reached over and clasped her mother's shaking hand.

"I became ordinary," Jessamin said. "But I had Oren once more, and as the last glimpses of moonlight remained, he and I pledged our love. Your grandmother married us right there, and he and I returned to Mooreston, where the villagers celebrated his return."

"It was worth the price," Bromwyn declared. "Love is more important than magic."

Jessamin squeezed her hand. "I did love him so. I loved him, though his time in the fey lands had left their mark upon him. He could not stand to be in crowds, and if too many people talked at once, he would scream. We lived on the very edge of the village, where our closest neighbor was Nick Ironside, the blacksmith."

Bromwyn had not known that Old Nick had originally been from Mooreston.

"There were times when nothing would console Oren, and he had to lock himself away until his sadness passed. Most of the villagers considered his strangeness a side-effect of his kidnapping—for the story was he had been taken by bandits and had been forced to travel with them before he could escape—and they cautiously accepted him once more as the apprentice weaver, and me, his wife, as a cartomancer. My magic was gone, but I could still interpret a customer's wishes and wants, based on their faces, their mannerisms, their way of speaking." Jessamin smiled briefly. "And I could talk a good game, if needed."

Rusty would have thoroughly approved. Bromwyn grinned.

"Soon we had you." Her mother smiled again, warmer this time. "Oh, how Oren loved to hold you. You soothed him in ways that even I could not. You made him better, Daughter. You healed him with a laugh."

Bromwyn blinked away sudden tears. How she wished she could remember her father!

Her mother's smile faded. "You do not know the people of Mooreston. They are a suspicious people, and they look unfavorably upon anything that hints at magic. Old Gilla there is known simply as Mistress Midwife, and she and her apprentice work their craft in secret. Everyone there knocks on Gilla's door when they need a tonic for one ailment or another, but they would burn her alive if they thought her a witch."

Horrified, Bromwyn said, "Truly?"

Jessamin nodded. "Most had accepted your father's oddness. But some—" Her voice broke, and she cleared her throat before she continued. "Some did not accept it. They saw my work with the cards as deviltry, and soon they whispered that my evil had enchanted Oren." Her hand, still in Bromwyn's, shook violently. "They came for us at night. They entered our home and slew your father. They would have killed you and me as well, had Nick Ironside not arrived, swinging his axe. He dispensed justice that night, but even so, I lost Oren again—this time, forever."

"Oh, Mother," Bromwyn cried. "I am so sorry!"

"Old Nick decided to leave Mooreston, and we left with him. The three of us came to Loren, where they were in want of a blacksmith. When I became Mistress Cartomancer, the people here assumed that cartomancy was what I had studied with Niove Whitehair for all those years. None truly remembered that I had once been a witch. In truth, I had never acted the part." A bitter smile played on her face. "The people of Loren remembered a carefree, irresponsible girl, and they saw before them a new widow with a baby. I told them only that my husband had drowned. Old Nick never said otherwise. He remained a good friend to me over the years, though he never attempted to court me. I think he knew it would not have mattered. My heart had broken and turned to stone the night your father died. And one can never mend a heart of stone."

Jessamin lowered her head and sighed deeply.

"The fey had taken my love and returned my love at the cost of my magic," she rasped. "And then I lost my love once more because of the fey's mark upon him. And today, I spoke of things I had sworn never to speak of because the fey tricked you into thinking their foul blood runs in your veins." She squeezed her daughter's hand once more, then pulled away.

"Mother," Bromwyn said, her voice breaking. "Please forgive me. I did not realize."

Jessamin glanced down at her lap. "Tell me, Daughter: Your friend, the one whom your grandmother tricked into becoming the Guardian—did he go unchallenged?"

Bromwyn bit her lip before she replied, "No."

"Did the fey take him?"

"No," she said again. "I saved him."

After a pause, her mother replied, "That is good."

Bromwyn went to Jessamin's side and knelt beside her, imploring. "I love him, Mother. I would lose everything if it meant having just him. Please, I beg you: Release me from my marriage promise."

"Love scars you, my daughter. I would spare you from that pain."

"It is a pain I am willing to have."

"You need protection."

"Mother," Bromwyn said quietly, "when you were married, did that protect you?"

In reply, tears spilled down Jessamin's cheeks.

"Please," Bromwyn whispered. "Please."

For a long moment, Jessamin did not speak. And then, through her tears, she replied, "If your grandmother agrees, then yes, I will end your betrothal."

Bromwyn sobbed with relief as she hugged Jessamin tightly. "Thank you," she whispered, and "thank you," and "thank you" again, and for a time, the air was filled with thanks and quiet sobs.

Finally, Bromwyn gently kissed Jessamin's brow. "I must go," she said. "Grandmother is expecting me, and now I have even more reason to go there quickly."

Her mother nodded and brushed away her tears. "Go. And Daughter?"

"Yes?"

"Everything I have done has been for love. And it ended poorly." Her voice broke. "You are a better witch than I have been. Be better at love too."

"I will," Bromwyn promised, and then she kissed her mother once again before she ran out the door.

# ONE NIGHT'S ACTIONS

Bromwyn stepped quickly as she walked through the village, thinking of what words could sway her grandmother into breaking off the engagement. Surely, even the witch of the Way of Death had to bow her head before love. Surely.

Bromwyn pondered and walked faster.

As she hurried, she noted that the people of Loren had clearly been working for hours, cleaning up the mess the fey had left in their wake: A massive pile of wreckage had been gathered in the Village Circle, and it slowly grew larger as one by one, villagers added shattered furniture and broken tools to the mound. Men and women and children all worked together, sweeping and hauling and gathering and, in the case of livestock, catching. Stray sheep trotted along the avenue, sporting colors upon their coats that would have put Mistress Dyer out of work. The heavy smell of charred wood and scalded grain still hung in the air, but based on the gathering clouds, the coming summer rain would soon set it right. Stepping quickly and carefully in the muddy streets, Bromwyn nodded to the villagers as she strode past.

And if one or two of them bowed their heads and murmured "Wise One," well, who was she to tell them otherwise?

She paused by the ruins outside of the bakery, where she saw a familiar, red-haired boy hauling debris as his parents loaded the ovens. The sight of Rusty doing an honest day's work made her smile. Perhaps the thief prince could learn after all. Seeing him made her heart swell, and she quickened her pace to a run. Surely, she could get her grandmother to see reason.

"Lady Witch," a man's voice called.

She halted her steps and turned to see Brend approaching her.

"Sir Smith," she said, surprised. During the year of their betrothal, he had never willingly spoken with her. "You look well, considering your ordeal last night."

He smiled awkwardly, just a flick of his mouth, but it was enough to soften the hard lines of his face. "A black eye or two is nothing. I get worse every day from the forge."

She recalled seeing his naked back, broad and muscular and peppered with fine scars. "If I may pry, is everything right again between you and your master?"

"He bent over backward to apologize. Said he wasn't himself last night. And that was plain to anyone who knows him. He's a good master and a good man."

"Just this morning, my mother told me something similar."

Bromwyn smiled. "I am glad Nick Ironside made amends with you."

"Yes. Well. So. I've been thinking. I never thanked you. For what you did last night." He took a breath. "Thank you."

Bromwyn's mouth opened and closed, then opened once more, and she found her voice. "You are very welcome."

He nodded, looking relieved. "I have to get back, keep helping with the cleanup. Fairies made a mess of things. Fairies," he said again, quieter, shaking his head.

"And my grandmother is expecting me. Oh, Sir Smith—"

"Brend," he rumbled, and then he coughed. "Given that we're to wed, it seems you should call me Brend."

"Brend," she agreed, "this should please you: After I speak with my grandmother, we can end our betrothal! We will not be forced to marry," she said happily. "My mother finally understands that this would be a poor match, and she is willing to relent. I am certain my grandmother will agree. And once that is done, we will be free!"

"Well," Brend said, blinking his blackened eyes. "Yes, good. Well then." He cleared his throat. "Good luck to you, Lady Witch."

"If you are Brend, then I am Bromwyn."

"Bromwyn. Yes." He half-turned, then he faced her once more. "If the Wise One doesn't agree and the wedding remains set, then you and I, we'll just have to make the best of it. This match may be not as terrible as we thought."

Her eyebrows nearly flew off her face. "Of course it is! You think my craft is deviltry!"

"Your deviltry saved my life."

"And that makes a difference?"

His awkward smile returned briefly, there and gone again. "One night's actions can change everything."

A torrent of emotions battered her, anger and flattery and others that were too quick for her to name. Here was the man who, as a child, had turned his back on her. Here was her betrothed who, just yesterday, thought her magic was unnatural.

And, just yesterday, her grandmother still possessed the Key to the World Door. Yesterday, Bromwyn and her mother still clawed at each other like cats.

Yesterday, Bromwyn had not known that Rusty loved her, or realized that she loved him.

She calmed herself, and she conceded, "Many things can happen in one night, but ... Brend, you should know that I love someone else."

There was a pause, and then he shrugged. "I didn't say it would be a perfect match. Just not as terrible as we'd thought. Go on, speak to the Wise One. Who knows? Maybe she'll do as you hope."

She saw the skepticism in his eyes. "You think she will not."

"The Wise One can be ... " He groped for the right word. "Stubborn."

"So can I."

Another pause; another hint of a smile. "Your daily visits at the forge are proof of that." He sketched a bow. "Until tomorrow, Lady Witch."

Bromwyn smiled ruefully. "Until then, Sir Smith."

She watched him go, and then, as she continued on the way to her grandmother's cottage, she thought that perhaps Nick Ironside had taught his apprentice more than the art of forging.

# APPRENTICED NO MORE

Bromwyn found her grandmother outside of her cottage, deadheading the lilacs.

Niove, wearing a wide-pocketed apron over her black dress, snipped the old blooms quickly, using her shears with a barber's precision. The discarded petals fell on the grass and streaked the vibrant green with shades of purple. When Bromwyn was younger, she hadn't understood why lilacs needed to be pruned; to her, it had seemed as if her grandmother was maliciously killing the flowers. It was only once she had become Niove's apprentice that she learned about gardening in general and pruning in particular. Cutting away dead things helped make live things grow. When Bromwyn had asked if that meant one day, her mother's hair would grow long again and she'd find her magic, Niove had replied, "No amount of tending will help that particular garden. Dead is dead."

And of course, her grandmother would know all about *that*.

Now, in her garden, Niove spoke idly to the flowers that she snipped. "Some children are taught not to speak unless spoken to. I think that is a ridiculous custom, although one can learn to appreciate the quiet. Do not just stand there, girl. Make your manners."

Bromwyn rubbed her ear as if her grandmother had just clouted it. "Grandmother, I—"

"And that is what you call 'manners,' I suppose." Niove sighed. "Then again, I should expect no less from one who greets the fey rulers while barefoot."

"Good afternoon, Grandmother," Bromwyn said loudly, fixing a smile on her face.

"And now she thinks I am deaf. Wheel and want." Niove shook her head and finally glanced at her granddaughter. "I expected you sooner."

"Mother insisted that I bathe."

"And you actually listened?"

"She threatened to scrub me herself."

"Heh." Niove turned back to the flowers. "So you passed your test. Congratulations."

Bromwyn shifted her feet. "You do not sound pleased."

"Oh, I am quite pleased. It shows that you were not a complete waste of my time. Though based on you forgetting more than you remembered last night, it also shows that your head is not as big as you think it is." She slid Bromwyn a glance. "How many called you 'Wise One' today? And how many did you correct?"

Bromwyn blushed.

"I thought as much. It is fine for the villagers to think you are above your station and act accordingly. But do not forget where you truly stand."

"And where is that, Grandmother?"

"In my garden, at the moment."

Bromwyn bit her lip. "What I meant to say was, what happens now? Am I still your apprentice, now that I am a full witch of the Way of Sight?"

Her grandmother cut off another bloom. "You are no such thing."

Bromwyn's mouth worked silently.

"Close your mouth, girl." Niove put her shears into her apron pocket, and then she turned to face her granddaughter. "Tell me this: What was your test?"

"I helped the Guardian—"

"Do not be daft. I did not ask what you *did*. Tell me exactly *how* you were tested."

"I ... I do not know," she said meekly.

Niove let out a long-suffering sigh. "At least you admit when you do not have an answer. You broke your curse."

At first, Bromwyn didn't know what that had to do with her test—and then she understood. "Breaking the curse was my test!"

"I just said that. What did you offer the fey before you finally realized why you were offering it in the first place?"

"Myself," she said, frowning as she remembered what had happened in the shadow of the World Door. "I begged them to take me instead of Rusty."

"The boy failed the challenge? And here I thought he actually had a brain somewhere beneath that ridiculous hat of his. Well. You offered yourself to the tender mercies of the fey. Yes, that would indeed be self-sacrifice. Well done." Niove smiled, then—a proud smile that Bromwyn had rarely seen.

"Thank you," Bromwyn murmured, pleased and embarrassed and not quite knowing how to react.

"So you are the Guardian now, eh? The Queen must have pitched a fit. That one does not care for it when those she has her eye on manage to slip away."

"She was quite angry," Bromwyn said, allowing herself a smile. Then she remembered the King's final words to her, and her smile fell away from her face. "The King as well. He has promised to challenge me next year."

Niove waved her dismissal. "That one is more than full of himself. He challenged me more times than I can count, for all the good that did him."

Bromwyn remembered the hunger in the King's eyes, and his promise that next Midsummer, her life would be his. She swallowed, and she told herself to stop being a fool. To bolster her courage, she said, "He told me his name, Grandmother."

"Did he? You must have made quite the impression. Very good, Bromwyn."

She grinned.

"Did the lady Queen share her name as well?"

The grin faltered. "No."

"Well, there you go: You have a goal for next Midsummer. The Key is safe, I take it?"

She took the iron key out of her pocket and showed it to her grandmother.

"Nature's grace, girl—do not carry the thing with you all the time!" Niove sniffed. "I hear there are thieves in the village."

Bromwyn sighed. "Indeed."

"So what did they tell you? Do not look so surprised; those two always prod and poke, telling half-truths mixed with lies, just to get a reaction. What did they say to you?"

"They made horrible insinuations about Mother, even going so far as to say I had fey blood in my veins." Bromwyn laughed uneasily. "I should not have given the lie any thought at all, but I admit, they made me doubt."

"Oh, that was no lie."

Bromwyn's eyes nearly popped out of her skull.

"An exaggeration, maybe. But no lie." Niove mumbled words from her Way, and the ground answered her with a rumble. A tree stump erupted, blackened and shedding soil, and she slowly eased herself onto it. "Ah, much better. Has your mother told you the truth of it about your father?"

"Just … just this morning," Bromwyn stammered.

"Oren Moon was a fool and a dreamer," Niove said, "but his heart was good, and that matters more than the first two things combined. When he vanished, I thought that might be the death of your mother." She rolled her eyes. "That girl was as heartblind as they come. Her Way's fault, I suppose. Me, I do not have any

257

patience for the Way of the Heart. Emotions are messy, even when magic does not come into play. She begged me to bring him back from the dead when everyone thought he had drowned."

"Would you have?" Bromwyn asked softly. "Had he been dead, I mean. Would you have returned him to her?"

Niove eyed her. "Dead is dead, and not meant to breathe among the living. But he was not dead. He had been lured into a waygate in the river, and he was taken to the fey lands."

"Mother told me."

"Indeed? Did she also tell you what happens to mortals when they walk beneath the cold sun of the fey lands?"

Bromwyn's brow crinkled. "No."

"They become fey themselves. It is a slow process, and a painful one. By the time your father returned through the World Door, fey magic had burrowed into his blood. His time there changed him." Niove grimaced. "Mortals are not meant to walk the immortal lands."

"Then—" Bromwyn's voice cracked. "Then they told me the truth. I *am* fey."

Her grandmother snorted. "You are as human as I am, girl. But the magic that flows within you, that is a little stronger than that of most other witches. A little wilder. It lets you walk paths that others could not, not without burning out."

Bromwyn thought of what she had done with Master Tiller's fields, thought of how she had accidentally spelled her mother years ago and caused Jessamin to age. "So ... does that mean I am *not* a witch of the Way of Sight?"

"Every witch is more than just her specific Way."

"But you are a witch of the Way of Death."

"I am also the Wise One of Loren, and the mother of Jessamin Moon, and your grandmother, and so much more." Niove chuckled. "Granted, most people hear the part about 'death,' and that is as much as they are willing to hear. Perhaps you thought you were bound to the Way of Sight, and if I gave you that impression, well, that was to help keep you from experimenting with magic too strong for you to handle." Niove arched an eyebrow. "Which, of course, did not stop you from doing exactly that. Spelling your clothing to keep cool in the summer and warm in the winter? Have you never heard of dressing appropriately for the weather?"

Bromwyn's cheeks burned, and she bit her lip.

"You are a witch, and suffice it to say that you are no longer an apprentice. There will be time enough for you to declare your Way of Witchcraft; that time is not now. Do not fence yourself in, not when you are first about to explore."

"I do not want to be fenced," Bromwyn said, seeing her chance. She steeled herself, and she said, "Grandmother, I do not want to marry Brend Underhill."

"This again?" Niove rolled her eyes. "I have heard this tale before. Tell the bard to sing another."

"Please, Grandmother—I do not love him."

"Yes, I know, you love your friend who thinks himself a thief; otherwise, the curse would not have broken. What of it?"

"Mother has agreed to call off my engagement, as long as you give your consent."

"The blacksmith boy is a better match for you than your thief."

Bromwyn's chest tightened. "Grandmother … "

"Granted, the blacksmith does not have much sense to him, but who needs sense to swing a hammer? Not that the thief is any better. He should know that sticky fingers can be easily chopped off."

Bromwyn felt her freedom slipping away. She whispered, "Please."

"Humph. You and your mother both, so easily swayed by love." Niove stood, and the tree stump sank back into the ground, which filled in until there was no hint of where the stump had been. "And look how well that turned out for her."

Bromwyn blurted, "Please! Do not force me to marry the wrong man!"

"Who is forcing you to do anything? Is there some knife at your throat that I cannot see?"

"I am bound by Mother's promise to the Underhills," Bromwyn cried. "As you well know!"

"Are you? Why do you not simply run off with that thief boy you claim to love?"

Bromwyn blinked. "Why … because I am to be the Wise One of Loren. I cannot simply run away."

"So you do understand responsibility. For a moment, I was not so sure." Her grandmother glanced up at the sky. "The rains are coming. Just as well. The land could use a scrubbing after Midsummer."

"Grandmother … "

Niove adjusted her black shawl. "So. Your test is done. You are an apprentice no longer. Now you are a journeywoman, ready to travel different paths until you find the one that will lead you to becoming a master of a Way of Witchcraft."

Bromwyn clenched her teeth. "But what of the engagement? You would leave me trapped in a marriage I do not want?"

"Listen to the girl, saying she is trapped." Niove shook her head. "Your problem, Bromwyn, is that you are seeking to escape, when all you need to do is walk out. You of all people should have learned that particular lesson very well," she said dryly.

"But … "

"Who has been insisting that you are trapped?"

Flustered, Bromwyn replied, "I have been promised—"

"I am not speaking of promises made in your name," Niove said tersely. "Answer my question, girl: Who says that you are trapped?"

Bromwyn paused. "I do."

"Then do not be trapped. It is as simple as that."

*Do not be trapped.*

She remembered that Midsummer night from long ago, when a pixie had told her how to leave the cottage. She remembered her hand over the doorknob, remembered saying out loud that she was not trying to escape, which would have tripped her grandmother's spell—she was simply walking out. And so she had. After all of her sulking and screaming and seeking escape, it had come down to declaring her intention, and then doing what she said she would do.

She had decided, and then she had acted upon that decision.

Thoughts whirling, Bromwyn remembered all of the times she had argued with her mother over the past year. She had constantly told Jessamin that she did not want to marry Brend, that she did not want to be in a loveless marriage, that she did not want her mother to make this decision for her. She had complained and moped and fretted and cried, but she had gone along with her mother's promise.

Not once had she said she would not marry Brend.

Not once had she actually refused.

"Bromwyn," her grandmother said idly, "I believe you have something to say to me. I would very much like to hear it before the rain begins."

Bromwyn lifted her chin. "Grandmother," she said firmly, "I will not marry Brend Underhill."

"Finally! Wheel and want, girl, it took you long enough. Whatever else happens, you must always be responsible for yourself. Consider that your first lesson as a journeywoman."

Bromwyn's heart raced, and her breath caught in her throat. "Then ... you agree? You give your consent for Mother to end the engagement?"

"Yes."

Grinning like a fool, Bromwyn bowed her head. "Thank you, Grandmother!"

"And look: The girl has found her manners. Wonders never cease." Niove laughed softly, the sound like autumn leaves scraping underfoot. "I expect you back here tomorrow to begin your work as a journeywoman."

Still grinning, Bromwyn said, "Yes, Grandmother."

"And come early. No more sleeping in for you when there is work to be done."

"Yes, Grandmother."

"The rest of today is yours. Take it, and do with it what you will."

"Thank you, Grandmother!"

Niove Whitehair placed her hands on either side of Bromwyn's head, and then she gently kissed her brow. "Go back to your thief," she said. "You should run; the stories say that witches melt in the rain."

# THE LORD THIEF

By the time Bromwyn returned to the village, the rain had begun, a shower with aspirations of a summer storm. The villagers were undaunted by the weather; some had put up their hoods, but most simply allowed themselves to get wet as they continued their work of cleaning up after the fey rampage. The rain grew stronger as she crossed through the Village Circle, and the ground, still half-mud from the night before, attempted to grab her bare feet as she walked. The first peal of thunder sounded as she reached the bakery.

A small crowd had gathered outside the shop, perhaps lured there by the mouth-watering scent of freshly made cookies. Mistress Baker stood framed by the ruins of the doorway, and she held a large basket that overflowed with rolls and loaves and pastries. People shouted their choices, and the baker confirmed whether she had a particular item in her basket. One at a time, each customer put coins into the baker's free hand; the baker examined the coins, put them into a large pocket in her apron, and gave the customer the food just bought.

Bromwyn waited off to the side. Once the customers had all had their turns, a child with a dirty face and large hopeful eyes stepped up to the baker and piped, "Mistress Baker? I haven't got any money, but the cookies smell really good and I'm awful hungry." As if he had practiced it, his belly let out a large gurgle.

The baker sighed. She fished inside the basket and pulled out an oversized cookie. "My cookies are good indeed," she declared. "Best in Loren, and that's no joke. They're also the only bakery cookies in Loren, and for that, I'm grateful. Here. And if you tell any of your mudrat friends that I give out free cookies, I'll deny it loudly. Don't make a liar out of me."

The child squealed with glee, stuffed the entire treat into his mouth, and ran.

"And not even a 'thank you,'" the baker muttered. Then she saw Bromwyn, and she paled. "Lady Witch," she said breathlessly. She bowed her head and stammered, "Sorry, sorry, sorry. I meant to say, Wise One."

"Hello, Mistress Baker," Bromwyn said kindly. "I am still just Lady Witch. Or, if you please, Bromwyn."

"I wouldn't dream of being so familiar! I'm just the baker, and you're ... " She floundered. "You're the one that stopped murder from happening in the Circle!"

"Your son played just as important a role as I."

"My son," the baker said, and color returned to her cheeks as she smiled broadly. "So proud of him! Standing up to the mob last night—did you see him? Of course you did," she said, smacking her head, "you were right there! That was my boy, not afraid to speak his mind!"

Bromwyn grinned. No, Rusty had never been afraid to speak his mind.

"Before last night," Mistress Baker admitted, "I feared he'd never grow up. Hiding when there's work to be done. Dreaming about faraway places instead of being in the here and now. He's a bit of a scamp, that one. But then he went and did what he did. I'm proud of him, and that's no lie. My boy's on his way to becoming a man."

"He was very brave," Bromwyn said. "And not just in the Circle. Last night, he held his own with the fey King and Queen."

The baker pressed a hand to her ample chest. "*My* boy? *He* did that?"

"He did."

"Oh," the baker said, dazed. She smiled and blushed and smiled again. Then she frowned. "But look at you, getting soaked. Come inside this very minute. Careful of your step, though—the floor's still a fright, and the counter's been destroyed. Damned fairies. A menace, they are. Not the King and Queen, I'm sure, but the smaller ones, common fairies, I suppose you'd call them: nothing but trouble. They all but ruined our store, and they didn't even eat what we left for them on the stoop. Ingrates!"

She grabbed Bromwyn's arm.

"Look at those feet! Lady Witch, where are your shoes? Well, the floor's a mess as it is, so no worries there. Just be careful not to trip. Come inside!"

Bromwyn, who had been struck speechless by the baker's outbursts, let herself be led inside the store.

As they walked in, Master Baker, who was putting fresh rolls into another basket, shouted, "Kimmie, what're you doing? No customers inside! You, there, outside! Sorry about the rain, but the shop's just too much a mess to have anyone … " His voice trailed off as he recognized Bromwyn, and then he blushed furiously. "Wise One! Here in my shop! And with it looking like this!" He glared at his wife. "Damn me, Kimmie, you want me dead, don't you? I'm about to die from embarrassment!"

"You'll die of my strong arm if you don't shut your mouth," Mistress Baker shouted back. "Lady Witch here," she said, emphasizing the title, "wants to see our boy. Go haul him up from the storeroom, will you?"

Master Baker grinned at Bromwyn, then frowned at his wife. "Will you at least feed the girl? She looks like she hasn't eaten in a year."

"Charlie! Get the boy!"

"I'm going! I'm going!" And he went, grumbling.

"Forgive him," said Mistress Baker. "He says things before he thinks. He's a man. Can't be helped."

Bromwyn burst out laughing.

"Here, now, this is for you. Your favorite, if I remember correctly." From her large basket, the baker took out a sugar cookie and gave it to Bromwyn. "Eat up now."

"I am afraid I did not bring my coin purse," Bromwyn said, blushing.

"Like I'd make you pay, after the way you helped that boy and girl last night! I saw you, Lady Witch. You did a good thing. To say nothing of your helping my own boy. He told us a little about it— something about him getting into trouble with the fairies, which isn't really a surprise, since he and trouble go together like bread and jam, though I suppose the 'fairies' part is a little bit surprising if you didn't know any better. But of course *you* do, given how you were right there. He said he got into trouble, and he wouldn't have gotten out of it with his skin intact if not for you." The baker smiled a warm, lovely smile. "He said wonderful things about you, Lady Witch."

Around her cookie, Bromwyn said, "Thank you."

"Oh, don't thank me. He's the one who said them!" She leaned in closely. "Truth be told," she whispered, "I think he's sweet on you!"

Bromwyn didn't just blush; she felt her entire face go red. "I am sweet on him too."

"Wonderful!" The baker made as if to pinch Bromwyn's cheek, then thought better of it. "Lady Witch, if I may: My boy, he's got a good heart, even if he tends to be lazy. But he gets into trouble, as you know. Would you keep your eye on him? And if he gets in over his head again, would you help him?"

"Of course," Bromwyn said.

The baker dimpled a smile. "Thank you, Lady Witch. You've

made this mother very happy. Oh look, here's my lay-about of a son."

"Mam," Rusty said, affronted. "I've been working my fingers raw without a break!"

"Only because I threatened to chain you to the stove!" Mistress Baker harrumphed. "Go on, then. Take your break. At least that fool hat of yours will keep the rain off of your head. Hmm," she said, squinting out the window. "Actually, it looks like the rain's stopped for now."

"Thank you for the cookie," Bromwyn said.

Mistress Baker waved her off. "Go, go, go. The sun won't be out for long."

Rusty grinned hugely and nearly leaped out of the store, with Bromwyn close behind. They wove their way around the other villagers, finally coming to the cartomancer's, where Bromwyn led him up to the roof.

Alone, the two looked at each other, and then they both began speaking at once.

"Winnie, last night—"

"Rusty, I must tell you—"

They stopped, and laughed quietly, and then Rusty said, "I know it's supposed to be ladies first, but I have to say this now, Winnie."

Biting her lip, she nodded.

He took a deep breath. "Look, I know I said some things before the challenge yesterday, serious things, and I'd be lying to you now if I said I was lying to you then. But I don't want you to worry about any of that," he said firmly. "You're promised to the blacksmith's apprentice, and I'm due to wed the bakery, so that's all there is to it, and there's nothing else to discuss … "

In the space between him taking a breath and him babbling, Bromwyn remembered something her mother had told her yesterday, before the insanity of Midsummer had begun.

*When you love someone, you give up part of your soul.*

But it wasn't losing anything, she realized, listening to Rusty talk nervously and not hearing a thing he was saying. If anything, she was gaining from it.

Love was a silly thing. A wonderful, powerful, silly thing.

"Rusty," she said, "shut up."

And because he didn't, she decided to shut him up. Her lips fit perfectly on his, and for a lovely piece of forever, they kissed.

After, Rusty said to her, "Well, this makes a right mess of things, doesn't it?"

"Perhaps not so much."

"Oh, really?" Hope sparkled in his eyes. "Were you going to say something before you attacked my lips with yours?"

Grinning, Bromwyn told him that she no longer had to marry Brend.

Rusty whooped and kicked his heels in the air, and then he grabbed her hands and shouted, "A dance to celebrate this happy news!"

And so they danced across her mother's rooftop, laughing and thrilling in the moment. When they were done, they held each other closely. Bromwyn leaned her cheek against his, and she felt his smile against her skin.

"This," Rusty said, "is very good."

She murmured, "Very good indeed."

"You know, until your visit, I'd been having a bad day. I think you need to visit more often."

"As often as you like," she said. "Unless, of course, I am studying with Grandmother."

"Of course," he agreed. "If there's one woman I don't ever want to anger, it's your granny."

"Very wise."

"See that? I *can* learn." He kissed her again, just a gentle press of his lips on hers. "I have to get back. The shop's a mess—the fey really know how to leave their mark. Flour everywhere; sugar turned a color that I don't think exists. Whole thing's been quite the shock for my folks. They were lost this morning until I got started with the clean up. How they manage when I'm not there, I'll never know."

She grinned. "I can hardly believe my ears! Sir Baker, eager to return to work? Who would have thought it possible?"

"Maybe you've been a good influence on me."

"Maybe. Could I come with you, and help you return the bakery to its former glory?"

"Will you use your magic to make it go faster?"

"Maybe."

"You just want another sugar cookie, don't you?"

"Wounded," she cried happily. "To the soul!"

Rusty threw back his head and laughed, and Bromwyn thought

the sound the sweetest thing she'd ever heard.

"See that?" she said. "Maybe you have been a good influence on me as well."

"Maybe indeed." He offered her his hand. "Shall we?"

She entwined her fingers around his. "Yes."

As they started to walk, he said, "Winnie?"

"Yes, Rusty?"

"I love you, Lady Witch."

With a smile, she replied: "And I love you, Lord Thief."

She could think of no better title for him, for, in truth, he had stolen her heart.

# ACKNOWLEDGEMENTS

This book was a very (very) long time in coming. It started as a short story and eventually grew into the full-length novel that it is today. This never would have happened without the help of many people, including:

Miriam Kriss, my fabulous agent, who has long believed in Bromwyn's tale.

Georgia McBride, my terrific editor, whose feedback helped me flesh out the story. (Go Hornets!)

The entire Month9Books team of authors and editors, for being so supportive and terrific.

Ty Drago, who cheered loudly the entire way.

Ryan and Mason, who don't mind when their mom has to lock herself in her office because it's time to write.

And Brett, my husband, my true love, who makes everything possible. It's all good, hon.

**Jackie Morse Kessler**

Jackie is the author of the acclaimed YA series Riders of the Apocalypse, published by Harcourt/Graphia. The first two books in the quartet, HUNGER and RAGE, are YALSA Quick Picks for Reluctant Readers; in addition, HUNGER has been nominated for several awards and RAGE is an International Reading Association YA Choice. RAGE, LOSS and BREATH are Junior Library Guild selections.

Thank you for reading TO BEAR AN IRON KEY.

Preview more great titles from Month9Books.

Find the diary, break the curse,
step through the looking glass

THE
LOOKING
GLASS

JESSICA ARNOLD

JEN McCONNEL
Nothing is more terrifying than the witch who wields red magic.
DAUGHTER OF CHAOS

# ENDLESS

## AMANDA GRAY